CRIMINAL
CRIMINAL

ALSO BY TERRA ELAN MCVOY

PURE

AFTER THE KISS

THE SUMMER OF FIRSTS AND LASTS

BEING FRIENDS WITH BOYS

IN DEEP

CRIMINAL

TERRA ELAN McVOY

SIMON PULSE

NEW YORK   LONDON   TORONTO   SYDNEY   NEW DELHI

SIMON PULSE

An imprint of Simon & Schuster Children's Publishing Division

1230 Avenue of the Americas, New York, NY 10020

First Simon Pulse paperback edition April 2014

Copyright © 2013 by Terra Elan McVoy

All rights reserved, including the right of reproduction in whole or in part in any form.

SIMON PULSE and colophon are registered trademarks of Simon & Schuster, Inc.

Also available in a Simon Pulse hardcover edition.

For information about special discounts for bulk purchases, please contact Simon & Schuster Special Sales at 1-866-506-1949 or business@simonandschuster.com.

The Simon & Schuster Speakers Bureau can bring authors to your live event. For more information or to book an event contact the Simon & Schuster Speakers Bureau at 1-866-248-3049 or visit our website at www.simonspeakers.com.

Designed by Angela Goddard

The text of this book was set in Adobe Garamond.

Manufactured in the United States of America

2 4 6 8 10 9 7 5 3 1

The Library of Congress has cataloged the hardcover edition as follows:

McVoy, Terra Elan.

Criminal / Terra Elan McVoy. — 1st Simon Pulse hardcover ed.

p. cm.

Summary: Eighteen-year-old Nikki's unconditional love for Dee helps her escape from her problems, but when he involves her in a murder Nikki winds up in prison, confronted with hard facts that challenge whether Dee ever loved her, and she can only save herself by telling the truth about Dee.

[1. Love—Fiction. 2. Murder—Fiction. 3. Prisons—Fiction. 4. Criminal investigation—Fiction. 5. Family problems—Fiction.] I. Title.

PZ7.M478843Cri 2013

[Fic]—dc23   2012022801

ISBN 978-1-4424-2162-2 (hc)

ISBN 978-1-4424-2163-9 (pbk)

ISBN 978-1-4424-2164-6 (eBook)

For my Spark

I'D BEEN DREAMING I WAS BEING CHASED BY A GIANT PIT bull. It was barking, and then it opened its mouth and I heard *Doooom. Doooom. Dooom. Dooom*, the bass beat sound Dee's phone makes. It was ringing somewhere on the floor, under our clothes. My eyes opened as he leaned off the narrow futon to answer it. We hadn't been touching because he can't sleep with anyone touching him. But I could still feel him moving away.

"We have to go," he told me when he hung up. He hadn't said much into the phone.

I watched the stretch of his ribs as he pulled last night's T-shirt over his head. The tattoo on his bronze chest disappeared: *N*—for Nikki—surrounded by swirling angels' wings. I smiled, seeing it. Thinking of my lips on it last night.

"Get up." He didn't look at me.

"Are you okay?"

"Get some clothes on." He walked out of the room. To the kitchen, or to find whatever narrow scrap of joint was left in the ashtray from last night.

I heard him muttering to Bird and her muttering back. Both of them low, short. I lay there hoping that Dee would say something to Bird about where we were going, what the phone call was about, but really I knew that hoping Dee and Bird would talk much to each other was like hoping the last scratch-off number on your ticket would reveal you'd won the whole $25,000 pot.

I kicked the blanket off and reached for whatever pair of shorts lay handy. I didn't know where we were headed, but wherever Dee needed me to be, I was going to go.

"I DON'T UNDERSTAND WHY THE *POLICE* WANT TO TALK TO you," I said to him once we were in the truck and he told me where we were going.

He just glared.

"I mean," I tried again, "how did they know to call you so fast?"

"It doesn't matter why," he said, working the tight muscle of his jaw. "What matters is what the fuck I'm going to say."

I tried to calm down my breathing, to think. *Jesus. The police already?* "Well . . . We were at Bird's yesterday. I mean, what else can we say?"

"We need a story, Nikki. Okay? What about after work Friday?" He was staring hard at the road, trying to burn it up with his brown-black eyeballs.

"You picked me up. Everyone saw you."

"And then?"

"The truth. We got beer. At the corner. We partied, slept over."

"We can't tell the police that."

For a second I didn't get it. Dee's almost twenty-one, but he's been buying me beer with his fake ID since we started going out the first time. October.

"But doesn't that make it more, I don't know, real? That you're being honest?"

He nodded just barely. "I'll think about it. What else?"

"Um, you spent the night and then—"

"Then I went to the gym."

"You went to the gym on Saturday morning like you always do."

He probably wouldn't tell the police how we'd also done it that morning: hot, ferocious, hard. And then again, in the back of Bird's car, after what happened. It wasn't their business. Dee didn't like to talk about that stuff anyway. But the thought of it still made me reach out, put my hand on his hard, narrow thigh. I didn't move my hand away even when I felt him tensing under my touch.

The next part was tricky. "Then you came back, and we . . . went to get sandwiches?"

His eyes flicked over to me for just a second. "Where?"

"Um—McDonald's. Or, no. Tell them the QT."

"The one up the street?"

"Yes, the one at the street."

"We hung out."

"We didn't go anywhere."

"Until we had to go get dinner," he said.

"Right. The chicken. I forgot. And more beer."

"We slept late this morning."

"At Bird's." I nodded.

"My phone rang."

"Your phone rang. It was your brother, telling you the police were looking for you. And we left right away."

His jaw, thigh, wrist on the steering wheel, everything was still tense. But he finally looked at me then. Really looked.

I WENT IN WITH HIM, SITTING IN THE WAITING ROOM, IN case—he told me—they wanted to ask me questions, too. There was no way I wanted to talk to the cops, or anyone, about yesterday, but the way Dee said it, I knew I had no choice. I spent the whole time staring at the floor, trying to slow down the red-swirling curls of panic behind my eyes. Nobody wanted to talk to me, though. Even though it took an unbearably long time, when Dee finally came out, he had that *Don't fuck with me* expression on his face. For the cops and me both.

We got in the truck without talking. I had questions—what he said to them, what if they wanted to know more, what I should do with the wigs and clothes, what was going to happen next—but he wouldn't even look at me, so I knew to keep my mouth shut.

He turned the stereo on, loud. Drove fast. He wouldn't answer if I did ask, anyway. Just pretend he hadn't heard. Or, not even.

When we got to Bird's, I wanted him to come in, explain how they knew to look for him so fast at least, not to mention why we went out to that house, what even really had happened, but he didn't even unbuckle his seat belt.

"Dee?"

"Go in and get the stuff."

"What are—"

"I'll handle it."

"Where are you going to take them?"

"Don't worry about it."

"That wig was expensive. The red one."

He turned to me, slow. Flat expression, like a snake.

The wrong thing for me to say. "Okay. You're right. I wasn't thinking."

"I need you to do a little more of that," he said.

Which made me snap. "How can I when I don't even know what to think? When you won't even tell me what really went on with those gunshots, and—"

"You know what?" he growled. "You're right. You don't need to think. What you need to do is shut up and just sit tight. Do what I tell you."

"Dee, I just . . . I mean, this is crazy. And I need some—"

"Look, I've got some things to do. I told them where we were, okay? Just like we went over. They won't need to know anything else."

He was already far away from here. But I needed him to stay a little longer.

"But what if they come and—"

"What if I put my fist straight through that mouth of yours, crush your pipes so you can't talk any more, huh? What if that? Okay? I said I would handle it. It's handled. You don't have nothing to worry about. Nobody knows what happened. I made sure. Now go get what I asked you."

He wasn't going to hit me or anything, but I got out anyway. When he was fierce like this, it was better to just disappear. Eventually he'd quiet down. He always did. And after, he was always sorry. Always wanting. And he needed me to understand this about him. I was the only one who did.

Inside the house, Bird was in the kitchen, mouth full of pins, pinching together white satin along the waist of her friend, Kenyetta. Kenyetta was finally getting married next month, and Bird was so excited she was altering her dress for free. I said hey to both of them as I walked past and went into the back room where I stayed. Last night Dee had thrown the bag with his guns, wigs, everything into the big wood-patterned cardboard thing I used as a closet. You were supposed to hang your clothes on this rod across the front, but it slipped out if you hung too much on it. Most of my stuff was in a pile at the bottom. But Dee hadn't bothered to hide that bag under anything. He just put it there, right on top.

Holding it, I thought for a brief moment about getting the red wig out. Maybe Bird and I could wash it somehow, get rid of any trace of him. It was pretty. And like I said, it had cost a lot. But I wouldn't have anywhere else to keep it except here. If I took it down the street to my momma's, she would just find it and wear it, and that could be a disaster. But more than that, I didn't want Bird connected with what we'd done. Dee said they wouldn't, but if they came here and somehow knew he'd had it on . . . I didn't want to picture what. Even if I wasn't supposed to think too much, I knew enough to know I needed to get all of this as far away from us as possible. I didn't want to open the bag anyway. I didn't even want to touch it.

Dee was more himself when I handed it to him through the driver's side window.

"I'll call you, okay?" he said.

"When?"

"Later. And everything's going to be fine. Don't worry. I'm glad you came with me. It helped, talking it through."

I couldn't help it. Smiling just a little. Knowing I was helping him.

"Okay." He nodded toward the bag on the seat next to him.

"All right, then. But really, when will I hear from you? Tonight?"

"Maybe. But, you know, it's not a good idea for you to call me."

I wanted to ask why not, but he was starting the truck up again, so I just stepped back. His face was apologetic. He really had calmed down. Before he backed out, he leaned out the window a little and tapped his finger against his lips. I moved in and kissed him—a peck at first, but then more. Like we were swapping strength. Strength to prepare us for whatever was coming next. When I opened my eyes, he was smiling at me.

"You do what I need you to do, baby. And I know that. Okay? And nobody's going to ask nothing else, I promise."

"Okay."

"I love you, girl. We'll talk soon."

Those words moving across his lips made everything turn gold. The insanity and fear of yesterday, of this morning at the police station—it faded into the background.

"Love you too."

He left. I stood at the end of the driveway and watched the black end of his truck until I couldn't see it anymore. Nobody was going to ask any more questions. Dee was going to get rid of the bag and everything inside. In a few days this would all be out of both of our minds. I hadn't seen much of anything anyway. We were going to be safe.

The house was dim inside, compared to the bright summer sun, and it took my eyes a minute to adjust. In the blinking switch over from outdoors to indoors, my vision was filled with Dee, running toward the Mustang yesterday. How . . . sexy and strange he looked. Running to me. And now he needed me to be strong and to help him. I was the only one—the only one—who he trusted.

"Everything okay?" Bird called to me from the kitchen.

I went in, said hey to her and Kenyetta, and scooped Jamelee out of her playpen.

"Just some errands we had to run." I lifted the baby over my head and bounced her, making her giggle. Mostly I was doing this so I wouldn't have to look at Bird, because she would know I was lying. "You want any lunch?"

"Girl, please," Kenyetta said from under Bird's hands. "Tyson on some crazy caveman diet before the wedding. Eating nothing but nuts and fruit. Plain steak. I need some carbs and mayonnaise, honey."

"We don't want to get you too fat," Bird teased, pinching Kenyetta's broomstick arm. To me she said, "We got about twenty more minutes here," before she frowned back at the dress.

I put Jamelee back in her playpen and went around to open Bird's cabinets. I took out some cans of tuna and Duke's mayo while Kenyetta and Bird got back to gossiping together. The sound of their laughing and jeering, mixed with Jamelee's squeals and gurgles, made me feel even calmer than kissing Dee had. Filling the kitchen with the smell of toasting bread was nicer still. Normal. I took a can of fancy green beans out of the pantry and threw those into a pan too, after chopping up a little onion and cooking it in some oil. By the time I was sprinkling pepper flakes on the beans and serving up plates, I was feeling more myself. I thought, when Kenyetta left, I'd ask Bird to show me what she'd bought yesterday on her trip to the outlets. We could maybe dress Jamelee up, take her out for ice cream. Everything would be fine. I would eventually stop hearing gunshots.

We sat down with our lunch in front of the TV. Kenyetta was in charge of the remote, flipping around, trying to find something decent, when she passed a news channel and then clicked back.

"You hear about this?" she asked me and Bird. "Yesterday? Animals, I tell you. They shot this man just in broad *day*. Coming home from some speech to Boy Scouts."

A wad of tuna and bread and cheese stuck, dry, in my mouth. I was afraid I'd choke. On the TV screen was the house we were at yesterday, me and Dee. The yellow one with the porch. In front of it were a couple cop cars and that CRIME SCENE DO NOT CROSS tape all around the yard. A news lady with wide brown eyes and straightened hair was talking into her microphone. Serious.

". . . still have no official suspects in the case, but we've been told by police that they have begun questioning a few leads in the investigation. Neighbors said they believed the shots they heard in the area on Saturday afternoon were simply kids playing around with firecrackers. If more of them had investigated those sounds, police might now be closer to finding the persons involved in the murder of Deputy Marshall Palmer, who is survived only by his sister, in Indiana, and his seventeen year-old daughter, who was out of town at the time of the shooting. A sad homecoming for her, for these nearby neighbors, and the county police force as the search continues for these brazen killers. For now, I'm Kelly Douglas, reporting live."

Kenyetta and Bird were talking to each other while the report was going on, but I heard nothing. Only the words of the news reporter: *persons involved*. Persons. As in, more than one. *Killers*.

Kenyetta's voice finally came into my head. ". . . know they ain't going to rest until they get these crazy-ass folks. Police don't take killing one of they own kind too light. Who I really feel sorry for is his daughter, though. Only child and they say she was up in Ohio somewhere looking at college when it happen. Can you imagine?" She put her hand up by her face like she was talking on the phone. "'Hello, is this Miss Palmer? We sorry, honey, but your daddy dead. You need to come back on down here.'"

Bird made tsking noises.

"They think a gang done it," Kenyetta went on. "Man's retired now, but they say he worked real hard getting the gangs out from over where all those, you know, refugees and them come in and ain't have nothing. He cracked down even on apartment landlords and all that. But still, son. In the *day*? Man coming home from his do-good work and just get shot dead."

"Lord, I hope we don't start seeing more of that around here," Bird said.

"You far enough away."

"These times, people getting desperate . . ." Bird went on, talking about the neighborhood, telling Kenyetta about the rash of break-ins that happened a few streets over from us at the beginning of the summer, but I stopped listening. I had to concentrate on making myself swallow the food in my mouth. On fixing my face in some kind of way that pretended I was as concerned about the neighborhood as they were. That my gut wasn't burning and hollow at the same time, finding out the man Dee shot yesterday—and killed, *killed*—was a cop.

Five minutes later, though, I was in the bathroom, over the toilet, retching. I'd said I wanted a shower and turned on the bathtub water, hard, so that Bird and Kenyetta wouldn't hear. I flushed and sat on the edge of the toilet, not sure I wouldn't puke again, hearing Kenyetta saying, *Police don't take killing one of they own kind too light.* Eventually I climbed under the water, my clothes still on.

Persons involved, the reporter had said. *Brazen killers.*

Persons.

Not just Dee.

But Dee and—

Me.

I WAS IN THE SHOWER A LONG TIME. THINKING, I GUESS, but mostly needing to get clean. I'd stripped off my clothes and left them in a pile on the bathtub floor, rubbing the soap over my skin, my hair, my face. Sudsy water washing down. I wished I could get it far enough into my ears, behind my eyes, to take away what few sounds and sights I had from yesterday, what Dee did, but I knew the only thing that would take care of that was time. More time, especially, in the dark with Dee taking over me—Dee and nothing else.

After I got dressed in dry clothes, I went into the kitchen. Kenyetta was gone, but Bird was still at her sewing machine. I walked past her as normal as I could and took a couple of garbage bags out from under the sink.

"What you doing?" Bird asked, not looking up from her sewing.

"I've done enough lazing this weekend." I forced my voice to be even. "I thought I'd do some cleaning up."

"Girl, you always welcome to it." She smiled.

"I thought maybe you could show me your haul from yesterday, too."

"Oooh." Bird let it out in a long breath. "We going to need a couple hours."

We smiled at each other again—I could feel how weak mine was—and I left her and Jamelee in the buttery kitchen.

In the garage, I found a rake among a few other rusty tools. I took it outside to the dried-out yard, even though there wasn't much in the way of work for me to do. At least there were enough dried leaves on the ground from the one little magnolia for me to push into a pile, plus those big grenade-looking pods. I raked them together as best I could, put them into my garbage bag. I also spent time plucking up the trash that people had dropped by the sidewalk on their way down to the bus stop—chip bags, Gatorade bottles, and grease-spotted napkins. Those I shoved into the bag too, wishing I'd thought to bring out latex gloves.

After that I set out for my real, intended task: cleaning out Bird's car. Dee had taken everything important from it yesterday, but that news report and what Kenyetta said scared me. Dee told me they weren't going to be asking any more, but I wanted to make sure that if they did come around, there wouldn't be anything else for them to find.

Besides Jamelee, Bird's car was her pride and joy. She'd bought it, cash, with her own money last year and had it custom painted so dark purple it was almost black, with a sparkly shimmer underneath the paint. There was a gold racing stripe down both sides and some Hindu symbol painted on the back that she told me meant "strength." She had it washed almost every week and drove it like a grandma, five miles under the speed limit. Though she was okay with me driving it from time to time, I knew better than to ask too often, and when I did, I made sure to keep it full of the expensive gas. She babied that thing that much.

Inside the car was a different story. Inside was where Bird let the chaos show in spades. The back was the worst: floor jammed with KFC bags and cups from Bird's other job, plus fruit bar wrappers and old Cheerios dropped by Jamelee. Receipts. Phone numbers for people Bird finished projects for months ago. Plus extra baby clothes (one tiny shirt with a big juice stain on the front), dried-out baby wipes, and even a pair of shoes I think Bird forgot she had. One single pink sponge curler, under the driver's seat, was so old it had a brown crust along one edge. I didn't know where half the stuff came from, and I knew Bird didn't either.

One thing I was glad I did find was a cigarette butt and crumpled-up pack of Dee's smokes. Bird would've killed me if she'd known I'd let him smoke in the car—even if I didn't really remember letting him do it—but now it seemed even more important to get it out. There couldn't be any proof he was in here. I shoved it deep under the rest of the trash in my bag. I almost wanted to text him, tell him what I'd found and how I'd helped, but he'd said not to contact him yet. I'd save it for a surprise later.

After I cleared everything out from the floor, it looked much better. I almost wanted to vacuum it out. But I knew cleaning it up too good would make her raise her eyebrow and wonder if something was up.

Whenever I got to a pause in the cleaning, I checked the glove compartment. Three times, four. Each time, I didn't want to even touch the latch, but I had to, just in case there was something left. But there never was, of course. Only the car owner's manual and Bird's insurance card in a little plastic bag. A flashlight.

As a last effort, I took the hem of my T-shirt and wiped off the steering wheel, the stick shift, and all the seats. I wanted to spray the whole thing down with Clorox, but Bird would think that was too strange. I kept chanting in my head, over and over, *Dee said they aren't going to ask us anything else.* And I had to believe him. He'd taken care of most everything. But now I was taking care of him—us—just a little more: the way he counted on me to. All that would happen now was we'd get further and further from this whole thing, and one day—maybe—I could forget.

CLEANING OUT BIRD'S CAR INSPIRED ME. AFTER I SHOVED
everything from the car deep in the trash barrel and put it on the
curb for morning pickup, I aimed for the back room—my room.
I tried to keep things decent in general since this wasn't really
my house, but there were clothes all over the floor and ruined
magazines, plus fast-food bags and trash from us eating dinner
in bed. Dee's ashtray needed emptying, and I knew those sheets
could use changing too.

"You sure you want me to interrupt?" Bird said at the door.
"You seem on a tear."

I tried to cover up the fact that she'd startled me.

"Feels good to make things nice, you know?" I was holding
a wrinkled pillowcase in my hand and worked at folding it into
a tidy square.

"Guess that was some date yesterday then, huh?" She stood there, easy, against the frame of the door.

"What do you mean?" Fold. Crease. Fold.

"You and Dee, all lovey-dovey. Like nobody keep you two apart."

"He's like that." I swallowed. "You just don't get to see him much is all."

She snorted. "Oh, I see him. But really more I mean you. Moving faster around the room all the time. Like something in you is on fire."

I thought I could tell her then. That she'd understand I'd had no idea what was going to happen when we left the house yesterday, what he was going to do. After all, she knew, from Jamelee's daddy, all about how you could think things were one way and find out they were another. She knew about doing what you had to do for what you loved most. But I also knew the kind of grudge she took hold of. And Bird already disliked Dee plenty.

"You just—take such good care of me, you know?" I said. "And I'm happy we could all hang out this weekend, I guess. I mean, it makes me happy."

Another snort from her. "You know I ain't never going to stop you helping me with the load around here." She smiled down at Jamelee, who had crawled down the hall to see what we were up to.

I swallowed. "I'd do anything for you, Bird."

Her gaze came up to me then. Probably it was my imagination, but it felt like her eyes were gripping me: seizing my bones and making my heart stop.

"Tell me what you think about these ridiculous curtains on clearance Mel talked me into getting, then." She laughed, picking the baby up from the floor and strolling down the hallway, leaving me with the pillowcase still in my hand and my next breath caught in my throat.

I DIDN'T LIKE GOING DOWN THE STREET TO MOMMA'S
house, but twice a month I had to. My stepdad Gary had told
that me turning eighteen legally freed me from her life, but he
hadn't ever explained how to shake her off me for good. Based
on the mail we got, he hadn't figured out how to himself either,
even from as far away as a twenty-year jail sentence he'd already
served five years on. This time I was doing more than checking
in, though, and taking care of the few bills there were to pay.
After Bird tried on outfit after outfit for me and dressed Jamelee
up in her new clothes too—both of them so cute and adorable—I
knew I had to get Dee's trash even farther away from them. So,
even though it was close to dinnertime, I told Bird I needed to
go down to my momma's. She shrugged and said she'd wait for

me to eat, and I left the house out the front door quick, grabbing the trash bag by the curb. Then I snuck around back and walked down the street.

Cherry, my momma, lived one block behind and two blocks over from Bird's place. She owned the house outright, thanks to my grandma, who had taken care of me once Cherry started her addiction for real. Of course, it wasn't until Grandma died that I realized exactly how much *else* she'd taken care of and what I would have to from then on, after. Thanks to Grandma's money, though, there wasn't a lot to pay for anymore, outside of food and regular expenses. But Cherry's and my phone plan had been linked for years, and even after I dropped out of school and started working at the hair salon, it always seemed too expensive or too complicated to change it. There was the insurance, too, which I knew from Grandma was important to keep up. I had let the cable get cut off, though. She could watch static over there, for all I cared.

Most of the house was dark when I got there, which wasn't a surprise. A single dull porch light on and one farther in the house—the light over the kitchen sink. I dropped the trash from Bird's car into the bin outside the garage and let myself in the back kitchen door. Right away I could tell Cherry wasn't home, though it wasn't clear how long she hadn't been. Around about sixth grade, when we first moved here, Cherry started getting . . .

sick. Sometimes she was sick at home, and other times she had to go somewhere else. How long she's actually been on drugs I don't know, still. When I turned thirteen, Gary went to jail on his Long Bust, and things got weird in other ways I couldn't put my finger on. Afternoons, Grandma would show up at school instead of Cherry, taking me over to her house to spend the nights that would sometimes last for days. Other times, Momma would be excited and in a good mood, and we'd have parties over at our house. Full of people. Usually loud and very happy. When she remembered in the mornings, she'd send me to school. Other days I'd be "sick" too and just stay at home and watch TV with Cherry and her friends. Lots of them men, like she had forgot about Gary altogether.

Grandma would cook me dinner. She'd take me clothes shopping sometimes. But then Grandma got sick for real, and I didn't see her for long stretches of time. I'd ask Cherry to take me to see her and she'd say Grandma was too unwell for any company. I thought maybe Grandma needed someone to care for her the way she'd taken care of us, but anytime I said anything, Cherry would get mad and say she wasn't the bad daughter I was accusing her of being. And then Cherry went away too, this time for five months. I was on my own in the house, but I did okay. I'd met Bird by then, and though she was five years older than me and could already afford to rent her own house, somehow we took a shine to each other and made fast friends.

By ninth grade, I had it pretty much figured out. I went over to see Bird more times than not, cleaning up and helping around in exchange for dinner or a place to sleep where there'd be some company. Grandma died sometime that year. Most of what I remember about then is that Cherry wore a yellow dress to the funeral. I was the one who talked on the phone to the ladies from church, coordinated all the casseroles that came to our house. Momma didn't actually *say* she didn't want to handle things, but she didn't take on anything herself, either. Grandma's lawyer called all the time, and I got so tired of telling him that Momma was still sick that one day I pretended to be her. I don't know if she remembers signing the papers. I don't know, still, if I did a right job in everything. But now Momma has her house and her own car, and though there's the insurance we have to pay and the phone, there isn't much else.

Finding all the mail was still a challenge. Sometimes it'd be in a tidy stack under a pile of CDs and dirty hand towels, other times it would be scattered from the back door to the bedroom, like some kind of treasure trail for me to follow. Today it was all in a mound next to the kitchen sink—a lot of it damp. Most of it was things neither of us needed to see, but I was the only one who was checking.

I walked through the bare, beige house to Cherry's room. After that time she was passed out in there, it was a habit in me to always check, before moving down the hall into my own room. Usually Cherry's door was open and the room was empty: her bed made or unmade, with her pale rosebud sheets. Sometimes just the mattress, bare. Maybe a blanket, bunched up. Grandpa's old desk cluttered with her various things. Wads of money sometimes, which I never touched. Clothes on the floor often, but other times everything picked up. Always the sense she'd been here, and hadn't. That other people had been here too, but weren't anymore. Today, there was an empty pill bottle just under the bed and two half-full glasses of water on the bedside table. I wondered the things I always wondered, and that never did any good. Had she been arrested? Was she in jail? Was she at someone's house—say Bo Jenkins's or Halfway Carl's? Had I just missed her? Had she walked out the door, ready for work, or cloaked in perfume and someone's arms?

Cherry. Her bleach-blond hair like mine. Her thin-lipped laugh. The way she sounded young even if she didn't look it. Teaching me to paint my nails. Yelling at me to mop the floor. Showing me how to pour beer for grown-ups—making sure the amber liquid went down the side of the glass so it wouldn't foam too much on top. Pressing a freshly hot iron against my forearm, her bony hand gripping down on my wrist, because I was sixteen by then, had dropped out of school, and wouldn't fork over my whole paycheck.

I went down the hall, past the dark, shadowed mouth of the bathroom, to my own room. We were like roommates, really, even when I was in middle school and Gary was here. Two girls sharing a bathroom, no real art on the walls, nothing that made this house seem like anyone's. Her toothbrush, and mine, in the same fluted glass from an old set of Grandma's. Both of us hostessing her friends in our nightgowns. Neither of us giving up all our secrets to each other.

Standing in the doorway of my bedroom, I looked around and tried to guess what she might've stolen this time. I had a fireproof lockbox in my closet—she knew it was there, knew she couldn't get into it, and sometimes this made her mad—but it didn't really matter because the things Cherry stole were strange. Months used to go by before I realized a pair of earrings was missing. Or a lip gloss from the back of my dressing table drawer. Gloves from the pockets of an old thrift store coat I'd hated. Once, a two-dollar bill that was pressed in a scrapbook, shoved under my bed since we moved here. I'd only noticed it was gone when I pulled out the album, wanting to show Bird how skinny I used to be, back before Grandma started feeding me regular. Before Gary got arrested and Cherry started getting really bad.

I didn't know why I was caring about it all now. It didn't matter what Cherry took from me. Now anything I truly cared about, I made sure to keep out of her reach. Including myself. And yet, looking down at the bed where she'd tucked me in, where some nights—even after I was too old—she bent close with her low-cut T-shirt and her lipstick and her glassy eyes, I felt some kind of . . . missing, maybe. Needing. Wanting her to somehow be different. To fold me in, hold me close, and tell me how she would make it all okay. But missing a momma you never had felt strange, too.

I went to the closet, the dresser drawers, to see if there were any different clothes I'd want to take. Most of my things had been moved over to Bird's, but there was always some leftover dress, some sweatshirt. I moved around the room quickly, ignoring the safe because it only had a couple crisp hundred-dollar bills in it anyway, and I wanted to save those, in case. I knew, at that point, Cherry wouldn't be home at all, but I acted as though she might be, at any moment.

TWO DAYS LATER AT THE SALON WHERE I WORKED, I HAD my gloved hands deep in relaxer when the glass door swung open. Coming in the door were two guys who were definitely not there to get their hair done. And I knew they knew. I knew they were coming to arrest me, and maybe Dee had been taken already. Panic washed over me and made it hard to stand up, let alone stand still. I thought of my phone, in my purse in the back room. Dee. I had to get to Dee. I tried to keep my eyes on what I was doing with this girl's hair, but all I could hear was their low voices, talking to my boss, Alessia, at the front counter. They said my full name. Nicola.

After a minute, Alessia came over and started putting gloves on next to me.

"Girl, let me take over that for you a minute," she whispered. "These men want to talk to you."

I couldn't tell if she was mad or scared or trying to help me. I took off my gloves, one by one. Trying not to go too slow. But trying not to hurry.

THEY DIDN'T ARREST ME. ONLY HAD QUESTIONS. QUESTIONS about my relationship with Dee, about this "Bird" person—what was his real name and could they talk to him. It made me mad, for a second, knowing Dee had said anything about her at all. But of course he'd had to. We'd talked about that on the drive to the station. And we had been at her house. I gave them her real name and address, thinking I'd have to call her right away when I finished talking to them. They asked me other things, like what was the name of his gym and what kind of car did he have. Those things were all easy to find out, so I knew I couldn't lie about them. I could tell from what they were asking me—*Did you know he had a gun?*—that they already knew enough anyway.

But they weren't arresting me. Instead they brought out this plastic bag with a crumply piece of notebook paper in it.

"Miss Dougherty, do you know who Nicole Palmer is?"

I looked at the paper. A letter. In Dee's handwriting. Words on it like *forever* and *baby* and *I will protect you always.*

Her name hit me. Nicole. Practically the same as mine. "Who?"

"We found this letter at her home. While we were investigating a crime scene."

Who? What? "I don't know who you're talking about."

"You don't know Nicole Palmer, who lives at 247 Abbey's Ferry?"

She *lived* there? "No, sir, I do not."

More words swim off the page. *Darling. My love. Never give you up.*

"And, Miss Dougherty, would you be willing to give a sworn statement here, telling us that Denarius Pavon was with you on August twenty-third and the twenty-fourth? The entire day?"

"Not on Friday, when I was at work. But he picked me up. We were together all weekend. And the morning of the twenty-fifth, too. That's when he got called and went in."

"All right, Miss Dougherty," the one who'd been writing everything down said. He handed me a card. "If you think you have any more information you'd like to tell us, you call this number."

I took it, but all I could see, as the detective put it in his jacket pocket, was Dee's handwriting on that letter: *You'll be my wife.*

ALL THE REST OF THE AFTERNOON, MY HEAD WAS FULL OF *my love* and *forever* and *Nicole*. That, and what would happen when the police got to Bird. Today she was at her KFC job that she did two shifts a week—Jamelee was at her auntie's—but I hadn't told them about that. All they wanted was her address, so that's all I'd given them. But they would be by. And all I could do was text her to call me, even though I didn't know what to tell her when she did.

I texted Dee too. He hadn't been able to call me yet, only texted a couple times since he left my driveway Sunday afternoon. It was hard, but I understood. The silence. There was a reason. This, though, he needed to know. *They were here*, was all I said. After an hour of not hearing from him, though, even that seemed like too much. Would I give him away somehow?

Mess things up? And when he did finally call, how on earth was I going to ask him about that letter?

I nearly burned off a client's left eyebrow I was so distracted, and at one point the fumes from the bleaching chemicals almost made me pass out. When everyone ordered lunch from Zaxby's across the way, I didn't eat. My mouth was full of ashes.

Bird still wasn't home when I got back to the house, and she hadn't called me. Neither had Dee. I let myself in, but then I didn't know what to do with myself. I stared at the living room, at Jamelee's toys on the floor and a big basket of laundry that I should fold on the card table. Mostly I had a crazy thought to pack my things, leave here, and run away with Dee, but it was like I couldn't move. I was just dumb, standing there, not even thinking anything really. Just hearing those shots coming from behind and to the side. Seeing Dee running between those houses, his knees high and his face blank. Picturing his handwriting, so tiny and careful, scratching out love messages to a girl who wasn't me. I'd known about someone else—one from when he and I were broken up before. But he'd never told me her name. That it started with an *N* too. Almost the same as mine.

The sound of Bird's key in the lock pulled me out of it. I heard Jamelee babbling and the rustle of bags and went to help Bird at the door.

"What's got you?" she asked right away, almost mad-sounding in her concern.

Which is when I started to cry.

"Lord, girl," I heard her mutter. I tried to reach for some of the bags to help her but she moved too smoothly past me.

I didn't follow her into the kitchen. Instead I plopped down, put my head on what clear space of table there was, and wept. I'd kept everything pretty well together since Saturday, but now the stress and the plain fear of it was leaking out. Bird moved around in the kitchen behind me while I sobbed, not even asking for an explanation. I remembered her face when she'd gotten home from her shopping trip Saturday afternoon and how hard it had been to not tell her right then. Dee beside me on the couch, his hand clamping down on my knee, the main thing keeping me quiet.

I knew it would make me feel better to say something to Bird now. For a lot of reasons. And yet I also knew I couldn't. Bird'd just go straight to the police. Or tell them when they questioned her, anyway. I didn't really know what might happen to Bird if they found out about us using her car, but I definitely knew what would happen to Dee if she told. The more Bird didn't know, the better it would be for everyone.

What I wanted—so bad—was to talk to Dee. He would be able to calm me down like he always did. He was always so reasonable when I wasn't. But I didn't know where he was or when he'd come back for me, and I had no idea what he was really thinking. After the news report, the questioning, and that awful letter, I needed Dee's strong arms holding me, his face filling up my vision, his body filling up everything else. He was the one who'd brought all this, and he was the only—only—one who could take it away.

BIRD FINALLY FINISHED WHATEVER SHE WAS DOING IN THE kitchen and brought two beers into the living room. Thinking about Dee, and knowing he needed me to be strong, had helped me stop crying. I'd smoothed my hair and I was sitting up, folding the laundry, trying to take deep, slow breaths. My hands were still shaking a little, and I was afraid if Bird saw, she'd come and say it out, straight: *Dee killed that cop, didn't he?* but she had her attention mainly on Jamelee, who was guiding herself along the edge of the couch. She looked over her shoulder every step or two to make sure Bird was watching.

"You gonna come out with it?" Bird asked me, still looking at the baby.

I stared at the side of her face a minute, not certain she'd actually said it out loud. And then she turned to me, eyes wary, but also worried.

Worried for who I didn't know.

"The police came to work today," I said slowly, hearing each word the way it might sound to her.

Her jawline tightened. That was all.

"They had some questions for me about . . . Dee. And"—I couldn't look at her, I couldn't—"I think they want to talk to you."

"Why? I don't know nothing about him."

Her voice dripped disapproval. Which meant I really couldn't tell her, no matter how scared I was. Telling Bird would mean terrible things for Dee. *What Bird doesn't know,* I forced myself to chant in my head, *isn't going to hurt her.*

"There isn't anything you need to know," I said, fighting to keep my voice calm. "It's just that we were here a lot over the weekend, and—"

"What did he do?"

Just like that. Accusing. Not asking me *did* he do anything, but straight-off knowing he was guilty. Automatic. Even if she didn't know what.

"He didn't do anything."

Even I knew it sounded untrue.

Her eyebrow went up.

And I don't know if it was the pressure of lying to her or of everything else, but that doubtful look on her face made me crack. I started crying again. At least there was one thing I could tell her about why.

"Bird, I know you don't like him, but can you just listen to me? For a minute? They had a letter. A letter from him. In his handwriting. And it was to this other girl. A girl Nicole. *N*, like me. And it said he—" It was hard to talk. "It said he was going to *marry* her."

I covered my face with my hands, finally really thinking about it now that I was saying it to Bird. Saturday, of course, but also all the other things leading up to Saturday. Things that hadn't made sense then but started making too much sense now. Dee gone for days this summer, me not knowing where he was. And then showing up without telling me, being angry, demanding. The strangeness of him showing up at all again in May—after we'd been broken up for almost six months. Saying, suddenly, "Baby," and "I was wrong." But never looking at me the same way he had before. Or at least not as often. How I felt, sometimes, that even when he was with me, he was somewhere else. Looking for some*one* else.

Now I knew it was her. He'd told me he'd gotten together with her after he and I broke up last year but that she'd ended things with him, and it was over. He mentioned her existence only once. And then, "She don't have nothing to do with us." He brought me that rose. He took me to get dinner. He spent the night here with me and Bird and he squeezed me close. He told me he loved me. Showed me his new tattoo. He'd gotten it for me—or so I thought—so I'd always be right over his heart. Forever. He was mine.

Now, sitting here, afraid and sad, with everything feeling wrong inside, I wondered if all along she'd known he was still hers.

I WOKE UP ON BIRD'S COUCH. MY CLOTHES WERE STILL ON. The coffee table was crowded with beer bottles—mostly mine. My eyes were half-glued together. It was starting to be light, but Bird wasn't up yet, and neither was the baby. We'd all stayed up late, thanks to me and my bawling. There was so much Bird could've said—would've had every right to. But her not saying it, and instead staying quiet, massaging my shoulders and neck while I sobbed—it almost made me feel worse. I didn't know how long I'd cried or how long she'd worked her slim, strong fingers into my muscles. I just know that, for a good while, every knot she worked seemed to undo more tears.

I shuffled to the shower, every part of me wishing I didn't have to go to work. But I didn't want to stay at Bird's either, in case the cops came. I didn't want her to feel like I was hovering around, listening. Or trying to influence her answers. And I didn't want them asking me anything else. Seeing that I was nervous. The honest truth was, she didn't have anything to tell them except that yes, we'd been here. That was what I kept telling myself. She'd left the house before we did, and we'd gotten back before her. So she couldn't say much. Still, Bird's dislike of Dee was sure to come through no matter what she said.

Thinking about what we'd told them, though, I started to wonder if maybe it was too convenient, me and Dee hanging out at her place all day, without her there. Maybe we could say we'd gone out somewhere that afternoon. The movies, maybe. Somewhere.

Dee. Had he talked to the police again himself? I still hadn't heard anything from him, even after I left for work. Panic squeezed me, picturing him arrested. In trouble. *Why* hadn't he called? I didn't know. I needed to see him. This was just too much. Seeing him would help me know. To know that I was overreacting, making up crazy thoughts, and that this—none of this—was really about that other girl.

NIKKI: They talkin' to B 2day

NIKKI: I 4got we went 2 the movies

NIKKI: Rmembr?

NIKKI: U ok?

NIKKI: D whre r u?

NIKKI: Can u call me at work?

NIKKI: I need 2 tlk 2 u

NIKKI: D?

NIKKI: Did u tlk to them?

It took him an hour to say anything back, and I was so high strung, I nearly dropped my scissors when the phone buzzed in my apron pocket.

DEE: *Breaking Hell*

I was so shocked to hear from him, it took me a full minute to realize that was the name of the movie we were supposed to have seen.

Of course the cops came later. To work. Of course they did. They talked to Bird around ten—she texted me after they left: POLICE WAS HERE—and then they came straight over to find me, ask me to answer some more questions. It wasn't much before eleven, I don't think. They weren't wasting any time. And they wanted me to come with them to the station.

I looked at Alessia and told them I had to work. They asked me when did I get off. I said four, and they asked could I come in then. Just some more questions, they said.

But their faces were harder than they'd been yesterday.

DETECTIVE: Miss Dougherty, we're going to need to record this interview so we can refer to it later if we need to. Do you have any objections?

ND: No, sir.

DETECTIVE: Now, Miss Dougherty, yesterday you told police that on Friday, August twenty-third, Denarius Pavon picked you up from your place of employment, Fit to Be Curled?

ND: Yes, sir.

DETECTIVE: Can you tell us please the nature of your relationship? With Mr. Pavon?

ND: He's my boyfriend.

DETECTIVE: And how long have you been together?

ND: Almost a year. But we were broken up for some of that.

DETECTIVE: Broken up for how long?

ND: Six months. Maybe less.

DETECTIVE: And you've been back together for . . . ?

ND: Since May, sir.

DETECTIVE: Three months, then. All right. Thank you, Ms. Dougherty. Now, back to the twenty-third. He told us that on that evening, he took you to pick up some beer and then got some food, and then you went to your friend Bird's, where you were all night. Is that correct?

ND: Yes, sir.

DETECTIVE: And Bird is Ms. Shondeana Brown, living at 173-A Harper Drive?

ND: That's correct.

DETECTIVE: Also, to the officers yesterday, you described the vehicle belonging to Denarius Pavon as a "black pickup truck, with black-tinted windows," is that correct?

ND: Yes, sir.

DETECTIVE: And what kind of car do you drive, Miss Dougherty?

ND: [Inaudible on tape]

DETECTIVE: Miss Dougherty, I need you to speak up, please.

ND: I don't . . . have one.

DETECTIVE: You live close enough to walk to work?

ND: The bus, sir.

DETECTIVE: I see. Thank you, Miss Dougherty. Now, after spending the night at Ms. Brown's home—do you do that often, Miss Dougherty?

ND: She's my best friend.

DETECTIVE: So would you say, you spend the night at her house more than . . . once a week?

ND: Yes.

DETECTIVE: More than . . . four times?

ND: It depends. Sometimes.

DETECTIVE: You work with Ms. Brown out of her home, don't you?

ND: Sometimes, sir. I help with hair, if her customers need it.

DETECTIVE: So would you say you spend a lot of time there?

ND: Yes, sir.

DETECTIVE: More than at home?

ND: You could say so, yes.

DETECTIVE: And does Denarius Pavon spend time there with you as well?

ND: Sometimes. Not always.

DETECTIVE: More times than not?

ND: I wouldn't say that.

DETECTIVE: But on the evening of August twenty-third, he was there with you?

ND: Yes, sir.

DETECTIVE: And also, according to your last interview, he was there with you all day on Saturday, August twenty-fourth?

ND: He went to the gym.

DETECTIVE: Is that a habit with him?

ND: He works out a lot, yeah.

DETECTIVE: Every Saturday?

ND: Mostly. Other days too. He likes working out. It calms him down.

DETECTIVE: And what time does he go to work out? More specifically, when did he go this past Saturday?

ND: In the morning.

DETECTIVE: Do you remember what time in the morning?

ND: Maybe like ten thirty? I don't know exactly.

DETECTIVE: And when he came back, according to his statement to police on the twenty-fifth, you went to get some more beer, and cigarettes up the street at the QT, and were at Ms. Brown's the rest of the day until you went to get dinner. You spent the night again. Is this correct?

ND: That's what I remember.

DETECTIVE: Well, Miss Dougherty, there are some things here that aren't lining up with what we've found. You're aware we went to speak with Ms. Brown this morning?

ND: Yes, sir.

DETECTIVE: And that she told us she was gone on the afternoon of Saturday the twenty-fourth, so she couldn't say whether you had been at the house all day or not. It seemed to her, however, when she left with her grandmother and her aunt, that the two of you were also preparing to go somewhere?

ND: No, sir.

DETECTIVE: "No, sir," you didn't leave that afternoon, or "no, sir—"

ND: No, sir, I didn't know she told you that. Until just now.

DETECTIVE: All right. You and Ms. Brown, you're good friends, is that so?

ND: Yes, sir.

DETECTIVE: And being good friends, she would want to help you out, correct?

ND: Yes, sir.

DETECTIVE: So, do you know why, when we spoke to her this morning, she couldn't verify the story you gave us? About you being at her house? But that she had the impression, from your behavior Saturday afternoon when she returned home, that something unusual had happened? That you seemed . . . excitable and out of breath?

ND: [Inaudible on tape]

DETECTIVE: Pardon me, Miss Dougherty, but like I said, you're going to need to speak up a bit. This isn't the newest technology, I'm afraid.

ND: I forgot we went to the movies. And to get something to eat. The movie was intense. I guess we were excited about that.

DETECTIVE: You went to the movies on Saturday, August twenty-fourth? And to eat?

ND: Yes, sir. After Bird left.

DETECTIVE: So, when you told the officers that you were at

Ms. Brown's house all day on Saturday the twenty-fourth, you had forgotten that fact?

ND: Yes, sir.

DETECTIVE: Miss Dougherty, had you been drinking on the twenty-fourth?

ND: Y-yes, sir.

DETECTIVE: And the night before?

ND: Yes, sir.

DETECTIVE: And, as you've said, your memories of that weekend are a little unclear?

ND: I don't—

DETECTIVE: Forgetting the movies, for example?

ND: I guess so, sir.

DETECTIVE: Do you remember what movie you saw that day?

ND: *Breaking Hell.*

DETECTIVE: Was it good?

ND: It was all right.

DETECTIVE: And when you went to eat, was that before the movie or after?

ND: It was . . . before.

DETECTIVE: Can you tell me where that was?

ND: There was a McDonald's nearby.

DETECTIVE: Nearby the theater? Can you tell me which one?

ND: The big one. With . . . purple neon.

DETECTIVE: On Shallowford Road?

DETECTIVE: Miss Dougherty, because of the recording, I need you to say out loud "yes" or "no" when you're answering instead of nodding your head.

ND: Yes, sir.

DETECTIVE: And do you remember when you got home?

ND: It was . . . maybe . . . five? Four thirty? We got back to Bird's and then she came back, and after a while we had to get dinner. So, about then. I think.

DETECTIVE: Well, that certainly helps us, Miss Dougherty. At least with a few things. Clears up what Ms. Brown told us this morning, anyway. Now, about the QT station that Mr. Pavon mentioned. Remind me when you were there?

ND: Um. After the movies. Sometime . . . six?

DETECTIVE: So, early in the evening, then?

ND: Yes, sir.

DETECTIVE: And this is the QT station by Ms. Brown's home? On Memorial Drive?

ND: Yes, sir.

DETECTIVE: Because see, that's another difficulty. After Mr. Pavon told us you went there on Saturday, we went by there to check out their in-store video recordings, and unfortunately during the course of the entire day on the twenty-fourth, there's absolutely no record of either you, or Ms. Brown, or

Mr. Pavon coming onto their premises.

ND: It . . . might've been the Chevron. Or the Texaco.

DETECTIVE: The Chevron or the Texaco?

ND: There are a lot of places around there. Or—

DETECTIVE: Yes?

ND: I remember now. We got the beer when we got the chicken. Later. Because before that we were going to the movies.

DETECTIVE: And you got the chicken at the, let's see . . . the Kroger, you said?

ND: Yes, sir.

DETECTIVE: You're sure?

ND: I'm sure now. It was there.

DETECTIVE: All right, Miss Dougherty, thank you. I have just a few more questions for you, to make sure we have it all straight. Again, we appreciate your help in this. You said, both in your statement here and when questioned by officers on the twenty-seventh, that on the morning of August twenty-fourth, Mr. Pavon went out? To the gym?

ND: Yes, sir.

DETECTIVE: And the name of that gym is, let's see . . .

ND: LA Fitness, sir.

DETECTIVE: Thank you, Miss Dougherty. So he went to LA Fitness, where he . . . has a membership?

ND: Yes, sir.

DETECTIVE: And he was back by, would you say, eleven? Eleven thirty?

ND: Something like that.

DETECTIVE: And it was after that when you went to McDonald's, and to the movies, but not the QT? I'm just trying to make sure. . . .

ND: That's right.

DETECTIVE: And did he go anywhere else without you that day?

ND: No, sir. We were at Bird's the rest of the time.

DETECTIVE: All day after he was at the gym, you were together? Did he go anywhere else on his own?

ND: No, sir, he didn't go anywhere else. We were together the whole time.

DETECTIVE: And you slept over at Ms. Brown's again, on Saturday night, the twenty-fourth?

ND: Yes, sir.

DETECTIVE: And on Sunday morning, Mr. Pavon got a call from his brother, which was when he took you with him to the police station. Is that correct?

ND: Yes, sir.

DETECTIVE: Did you have any idea why the police would call Mr. Pavon's house, looking for him?

ND: No, sir, I did not.

DETECITVE: Did you know why he would want to bring you with him?

ND: No, sir.

DETECTIVE: Do you know where Mr. Pavon is now?

ND: No, sir, I really don't.

DETECTIVE: Well, thank you, Miss Dougherty, for your help and your cooperation. If we have any more questions, we'll give you a call. And if you think of anything else—anything at all—about the night of the twenty-third or the day of the twenty-fourth, here's my card. You can phone anytime. Anytime at all.

AFTER TALKING TO THE POLICE, THE ENTIRE BUS RIDE BACK
to Bird's, my phone was in my hands, desperate to press the numbers for Dee's phone. Not being able to talk to him was starting to
be almost physically painful. The only thing that kept me from it
was the sense they could get your phone records and find out who
had called when. Dee would be pissed if I got in touch the second
I finished getting questioned by the cops. But I needed him now.
Needed. I felt like my entire body was vibrating with fear, and it
was hard to calm down. Sitting there in the station, talking to the
detective, all I could think was whether or not I needed a lawyer.
But I didn't ask because I didn't want to seem guilty. Or that I
knew too much. Also it was too hard not to just freak out at every
little thing, too hard to keep things straight. Like that business

about the QT. And them asking me about Dee's truck. How soon would it be before they were asking me more about Bird's car? And what, exactly, had they asked her this morning? What had they seen at the house? Had they talked to Dee again, like they did me? And what I'd said about where we went to eat, or what movie theater—was that going to end him up in trouble too? How bad was it, them checking the video at the QT, finding out we'd made that part up? What other videos would they be checking? How would we remember all of what we'd said?

I wanted Dee so bad. I wanted him telling me that it was going to be okay, telling me what to do next. Holding me, knowing he had put me through a lot. I wanted it back like it was on Friday night, before all this, both of us cheery and drunk, and then, after on Saturday—him so happy. And needing me as bad as I did him.

WHEN I FINALLY GOT HOME, KENYETTA WAS OVER AGAIN watching Bird do her cousin Teesha's nails at the kitchen table. It seemed like they might stick around for dinner, which meant Bird and I wouldn't get to talk at all. But maybe that was her intention. I couldn't tell anything about her because she wouldn't look at me.

I tried going back into my room, to listen to some music or read a magazine, but I was antsy. After not too long I lifted her car keys from the hook by the door and asked Bird if it was okay if I went to get some Coke, since we were out. Did she want anything? Her mouth twitched a tiny amount. She didn't look at me when she said we could use some diapers, too.

I hadn't meant it when I asked if she needed anything, and

maybe she knew it. I ran into the Kroger, quick, and almost grabbed the wrong kind in my hurry. After that I drove toward Dee's house. I'd only been there a few times, and then only for him to run in and pick something up—I'd never even seen his parents—so I turned down a couple of wrong streets. Each time it was more frustrating. Like the longer it took me to get there, the less likely he'd answer any of my questions. About the police. About that awful letter.

It was nearly eight o'clock when I finally got there. I was only sure it was his place because his truck was in the driveway and him, sitting on the front step, talking on the phone and smoking a cigarette. He was in a tank top, with shorts loose enough around his knees that if it hadn't been almost dark, I could've seen straight up. He looked quick at my headlights, glaring. Not knowing it was me. He clicked off his phone and stood, chest a little out and shoulders back. Hands loose by his sides and arms away from his body. Tough. I turned off the headlights and then he recognized Bird's car. But he was still frowning.

"What are you doing here?" He'd gotten to the unrolled window before I even opened the door.

"I just—"

He made a mad-sounding noise. "Don't get out." He pointed at me through the windshield as he moved around the front of the car.

"I didn't know what to do," I told him when he got in. "They found out we were never at the QT. And so many other questions. If I can't call you, how am I going to know what to say?"

"Back out. Drive. We can't be here."

"Dee, what did—"

"I said we can't be here. My mom, you know?" And I did know. His mom had a temper worse than his father's. Dee was always getting in fights with her. I'd heard a few on the phone. One time he had this huge bruise on his back from when she'd thrown a hair dryer at him. Which I could relate to.

"Let's just drive," he said.

I backed out, not knowing where I was going. He pointed me along a few streets and then onto a dark road that passed by a post office. It dead ended at this science fiction–looking building surrounded by trees. There was a FOR LEASE sign in the grass out front. It was spooky, but at least we were alone.

"They asked me about Saturday," I started again. "Where we went. I had to tell them."

"What, exactly, did you say?"

"We went to the movies, like you and me said. The purple one—way out."

"You're right—that's the one we go to." Finally there was a little smile in his eyes, pleased with me. Proud.

"They asked me about where we ate. I said there was a

McDonald's. But I didn't exactly say we went in. Just that it was there."

"That was smart of you."

Relief and warmth gushed over me. But it didn't solve everything.

"Did you say anything else?" he wanted to know.

"Well, I mean, the gym. But that's where you went, so."

I saw the muscle in the corner of his jaw bulge, once.

"Anything else?" He was staring out the windshield now, not at me.

"Well, I don't know what Bird said yet."

His mouth was tight. "She don't know shit."

"No. You're right. But, Dee, they had a—a letter."

He turned to me, brows together.

I tried not to choke up. *My angel. Forever.* "It was . . . it was in your handwriting. To . . . to . . . another girl."

He looked away again. "That's old."

"They found it at the house. The house where . . . I mean, they were looking inside and they found it and . . ."

"I told you, that's old. She don't have nothing to do with us."

"But Dee, it was her *dad*! I saw it on the news!"

I was trying not to make him get angry at me for bringing her up, for not trusting him, but I was so desperate for answers it was impossible to keep from raising my voice.

All he needed to do was say again that it really was over with him and her. To fold me in his arms and tell me he was sorry I was scared. That there was . . . some other reason he'd done what he did to her dad on Saturday. A coincidence. Or, like Kenyetta had said, it was just someone his gang needed to get rid of, that was all. Not anyone who had to do with him and her. And me.

Instead he grabbed the top of my arm and pulled me to him. "Listen to me. You don't need to know anything about that. That's old business. You understand? All you know is, I picked you up on Friday, we hung out, stayed together on Saturday, I took you out, treated you, and we were together on Saturday night too. Even Bird can say so."

He looked at me, fierce, but then something in his face changed.

"I was good to you, wasn't I? Am good to you. I get you beer, weed . . . anything you want. And we had a good time that weekend, didn't we?" His eyes moved over my face, my neck, down to my boobs. When our eyes met again, I could see the full change in him. The want.

"Come on, baby," he said. "Don't we have fun?"

"But, Dee . . . they told me . . . her name. . . ." A tear slipped down. I didn't want it to, but I couldn't help it. "It starts with an *N* too."

I put my hand over the place where his tattoo was, and his

nostrils flared out, just briefly. Then his mouth was on mine, pressing and hot. Wet and full. Probing. Pushing me against the car door, hands up on my breasts, squeezing, lifting up, pressing in. His mouth on my neck, tongue by my ear, hot and swirling. Drawing chills up my arms and through my hips. It wasn't what I'd been looking for from him, but, as always, even against my doubt and fear, it was working.

"Dee . . ." Still, I wanted to hear it. I wanted to hear it was me and not her. The *N* was Nikki, not Nicole. But he was pulling at me now, trying to drag me across to him, and his hands were so hot. So hot, and so focused on me, my body. Me.

"Come on, baby," he murmured, stroking up under my shirt, squeezing my belly, my sides, then moving warm and hungry up under my bra. "I want you to forget about all that. It don't have anything to do with this." His hand slid down, finally, into my crotch, which was already pulsing.

"Let's get in the back at least," I said, starting to crawl over.

"THEY AIN'T HAVE CO-COLA ANYWHERE?" BIRD WANTED TO know when I finally got home. After nine.

"Turned out I needed a drive. Clear my head."

She was leaning against the kitchen counter. Her friends were gone. I moved past her like I wanted to get a glass of water, though mostly I was moving just to move. To keep her from looking at me too square.

"Yeah, I bet," she said quietly.

I could've asked, *What's that supposed to mean?* But she knew I knew what it meant. I stirred at the pot of collards she had simmering on the stove. I couldn't tell if she'd eaten without me or not. Most of the kitchen was spotless, which could mean one thing or another.

"Kenyetta and them leave?" I said, to say something.

She didn't answer. I changed my mind about water and went for the sweet tea in the refrigerator.

"You gonna tell me," she said behind me, "why the cops came to my house today, wanting to know about *Denarius Pavon*. Why he was at my house, and when?"

I poured the tea slow.

"I told you they'd be here," I finally said, not turning around. "I don't know what they want, but you know we were here." I brought the glass to my lips, even though I wasn't sure if I could swallow.

"Yeah, I know all that. More and more, though, I feel like there's things I don't know."

I faced her then, the rush of having been with Dee making me bold. His groans, his breath were still humming in my ears. My whole body was still wet with him, still electric and fearless.

"You know where we were," I said, cold. "And you know we love each other."

She snorted, turned to wipe the edge of the sink that didn't need to be wiped.

"You know," I went on, "that all I had before I had him was nothing. My job, maybe. You. You know he's been good to me this time around, has been here. You know you don't like him, but you know you can't say exactly why."

"Oh, I know why," she said, hand moving steadily. "Only I know you don't see it, so there ain't no point."

"What are you trying to say?"

This was the edge we usually came to, me and Bird. Fighting but not-fighting about Dee. About how she didn't like him, didn't want him around, but also didn't want to undo things for me—my happiness, mainly. It seemed like this time, though, there might not be a limit to her anger. No place where she might back off.

"I'm saying, Nikki, that boy ain't no good. And I don't like him in my house. And instead of getting smart about those two things, lately you just getting more and more up into him. Getting all wrapped up in what he is or isn't doing, with who. Some kind of letter, whatever. I'm saying to you, Nikki, that when the *po*-lice"—she slapped her hand down flat on the counter, making me jump—"come to my *house* and ask me *questions*, it probably ain't very wise or kind for you to take my car and go running off to him. I'm saying, maybe you need to think about who you really looking out for, and why. That's all I'm saying."

Her eyes were steel. I could hear her breathing through her nose, like a bull. But I think I was also hearing my own breaths, coming fast. It wasn't fair for her to make me choose. It wasn't fair for her to have this house and everything in it, her baby, her job, her life she'd been able to turn around because she was strong and smart and brave, while at the same time trying to keep me from having any kind of my own happiness. She *knew* I didn't have anything else. She knew it. And just because she didn't have a man, just because she worked too hard to ever meet anybody new, that wasn't my fault. It wasn't my fault my man came back to me and hers didn't. Wasn't my fault that she was too scared to love anybody—even, by the sound of her now, me.

"I won't bring him around anymore," I said finally.

She started yelling. "You already *brought* him around, Nikki! Him, and the police with him, and whatever bad he's done, trailing it in, dragging it around, and spilling it on everything in here!"

"I don't know anything about that!" I shouted back at her. "And you don't need to, either! What Dee's done is his business, and I trust him. I won't have him over if you don't want him here. But don't ask me to check my own happiness at the door too."

I was amazed that Jamelee wasn't awake and crying, the sound of us. I almost wanted her to be so that one of us would have a real reason to end this, to go and check on her and finish talking for the night. I wanted to get away from Bird, and her anger, and the lie she'd just forced me to tell her. I wanted to get away from police and questions and worry and all of it. I wanted Dee holding me again, like he had been only an hour ago. Making the world only him and me and nothing else.

"Go in there"—she gestured to the bathroom around the corner—"look in the mirror, and you tell me just how happy you are."

"Maybe you should do that yourself," I spat, turning around and leaving her there alone in her clean kitchen.

But when I went to wash my face and brush my teeth, no matter how hard I tried, I couldn't meet the eye of my reflection for more than a few seconds at a time.

Bird and I had fought before. Usually, after, we didn't even apologize. She didn't like dwelling on much of anything, but especially not ugliness. But apparently she'd been dwelling on her dislike for Dee even more than I thought. And now that it was out, I didn't know how long it was going to stay around.

The next morning, I kept out of her way. I was still mad too. She had to do her KFC job, though, and I had to go to work myself, so that made avoiding her easier. When I got home, we ate dinner at the TV and then went to bed, not talking more than we had to. I was calmer at that point, but it was clear she still needed space. I understood she was mad about the police, because they freaked me out too. But they hadn't come around to ask me anything else today, and I knew, now that she'd talked to them, she didn't have any more to worry about either. It was just like Dee said: they'd asked her what they needed to know, and that was the end of it. She was safe, even if she didn't feel it yet. We all were.

Friday I had off, and since I didn't have anywhere to go, I decided to try and make things nicer again between me and Bird. She'd been up early but lain down on the couch to doze while the baby bounced and squealed in her jumpy swing. I cooed and tapped Jamelee on the nose as I walked by, heading to the kitchen to make a big breakfast, keeping as quiet as I could so as not to wake Bird.

I made a mess of eggs and some ham, plus biscuits with gravy. The cooking melted away the rest of my upsetness with Bird. But even after the house filled with good food smells, Bird didn't come into the kitchen until I called for her. She sat at the table with me but pretended to be looking at a magazine while we ate. I watched her, disappointed that she hadn't even said thank you for breakfast. She wasn't letting this go. I cleared our dishes and tried to think of some kind of outing I could suggest, something fun for me and her and the baby. Something to help her realize everything was okay.

A knock at the door finally got us talking. Bird made a face, looking at the clock on the stove.

"Tyrone ain't supposed to be here for his suit until eleven," she said to me.

"I'll get it. Probably Jehovah's Witnesses, since the car's here."

She snorted, and the small laugh-noise felt like a kind of victory.

When I opened the door, I thought at first what I was seeing wasn't real. Two cops in uniforms, plus a detective in a suit—the one who had questioned me before—and another officer standing back, in the yard. Two squad cars behind them parked on the street, with a black police van parked farther down the road.

"Good morning, ma'am. We're here to see Shondeana Brown."

Polite as could be, the detective was. Like he wasn't turning my blood into ice.

"Who is it, Nikki?" Bird said, coming behind me. I heard her stop still, seeing the police.

"Ms. Brown," the detective said to her, looking beyond me. He held something up. "We have a warrant here to search your vehicle. We're expecting that you'll cooperate."

"You have a what?"

Somehow Bird was past me, on the stoop, jutting out her chin, looking fierce, even though she only came to the detective's chest.

"Ma'am," one of the officers said, his tone not as polite. "I'll ask you to step down, please."

I wanted to take her arm, pull her into the house with me. But I couldn't move.

Bird's hands were in fists at her sides, but her voice was low.

"Ain't no reason you have to be over here this morning. I already told him everything I know, which is nothing. You ain't got no need to search nothing of my property."

A small sound came out of me: "Bird."

The detective moved a step down, bringing him closer to her eye level. "Ms. Brown, a vehicle of this exact color and model—specifically, with the symbol there on the back—was described by more than one witness during one of our investigations. We noticed the vehicle when we were here questioning you the other day, and as this is—by your own admission and Miss Dougherty's—the residence where one of our suspects was staying, I'm afraid we do have probable cause to search your car. Now, I understand you're upset, but your cooperation would be appreciated."

I stared at both of them. Suspect. This man was calling Dee a *suspect*. I remembered his name then. DuPree. He was like this the other day too. Nice as pie. Like he was just coming over for a cup of coffee. And not in a fake way, either. In a way that made you almost want to do what he said. And now he was here. Here on our step.

Bird turned and looked at me, though she was talking to the police.

"Why. On earth. Would my car. Be anywhere near some 'investigation'?"

I wanted to sink into the ground, disappear. Bird's eyes on me, full of rage, and the lights on top of the police cars, spinning. They could be at Dee's house, doing the same kind of search. He could be arrested. There were witnesses. My whole body was water. I opened my mouth, but nothing came out.

"Ms. Brown, this shouldn't take much of your time. We'd appreciate it if you'd just let us begin."

I expected her to scream at them, throw herself in front of her precious Mustang, act crazy like a lady on TV, but she just made this defeated gesture toward the car and sighed. "Let me get the keys."

I hadn't moved—couldn't move, couldn't think, couldn't believe any of this. She got past me again, somehow, without even touching me. I heard her in the kitchen, the sound of her jangling key chain, murmuring to Jamelee. Lifting her into her arms. When she came back toward the door, I stepped out of the way. Found my voice.

"Bird, I—"

"You ain't speaking to me," she hissed, gliding past. She gave the detective her keys and then stood there, at the top of the driveway, watching them. Solid and unmoving, save to bounce the baby up and down a little. I wasn't sure what do to or where to go. Were they going to search the house? Had I really gotten rid of everything? I wanted to run to my back room, check everything one more time, make *sure* there was nothing, but another part of me—the truly terrified part—made me stay on the top step, riveted. Watching every move the police made: pulling on their gloves, sliding the seats forward, going through the compartments, opening the trunk, lifting up the floor mats, slipping their hands down in between the seat cushions. Even, of course, looking for fingerprints. A cold sweep came over me as I realized I'd forgotten to wipe down the car again after the other night. Would they find anything, or would it all just be a bunch of smears by now? Could they tell how old they were? Would it matter?

I was so tense, so afraid, that I nearly screamed when I saw the officer in the backseat drop something square and shiny into a clear plastic bag. Dee's condom wrapper. Shoved between cushions in the backseat after we'd done it on Saturday. The earlier one, from Wednesday night, I'd known enough to pick up and shove in my purse. By that point, I was on my guard. But this one—this I hadn't thought about. Maybe I'd been too freaked out then to even care. Too turned on to notice. But now it mattered. Now it could make a difference. Even after the officer put it away, it still stayed burning in my mind. Dee's spit could be on there, from when he tore it open with his teeth. Gunpowder residue from his fingers might have lingered—I didn't know. All I thought was that this was from Saturday, and there could be anything on it. Even the smallest thing could trace him to that day, that moment. To Bird. And there they were, placing it in that bag.

I almost fell to the ground. It was all I could do to stay standing up, to not plead with them not to take it, swear to them . . . what, I didn't know. The awfulness of what I did know—and what it would mean to Dee if I said any of it—was all that kept me shocked and silent.

THEY WENT THROUGH THE ENTIRE CAR. TOOK A COUPLE OF other things out, but nothing that stopped my heart in the same way that wrapper did. After, they asked Bird more questions. How to contact her aunt and her grandma, because they'd need to be questioned. You could barely hear Bird's answers, her teeth were clenched so tight.

She didn't stay to watch them leave, but I did, not sure they wouldn't turn around, ask *me* a few more things. But it was almost like I wasn't there. Not today. After they were gone, I stood there staring at Bird's car, wondering who had seen it Saturday. And what else they'd seen. I hadn't thought about witnesses, really, but of course there were probably houses full of them. It seemed stupid of Dee to take that chance, doing what he did in the daytime, but right on the heels of thinking that, I could understand why he did. The guy was a retired cop. Probably had a house full of guns. It hit me then that he might've even had one in his car. That Dee could've been shot himself. Hurt, or even killed. It had been smart, then, to surprise him that way. Nobody would expect a thing like that, in the middle of the day.

I was itchy all over to know if he was okay. I moved, finally, to head back inside. I would send a text. He might not like it, but I had to check in.

Only, the front door was locked.

I pounded the door with the flat of my hand. "Bird, I don't have my keys."

Nothing from inside.

I knocked again. "Bird, let me in."

The cold feeling I'd had before crawled back up into my stomach, along with panicky pricks all over. The locked door was probably just an accident, I told myself. I waited. I didn't have my purse, my phone—nothing. Maybe she was in the bathroom or running water in the kitchen, not able to hear me. I wondered what time it was, how long I might have to be out here until Tyrone arrived.

I knocked hard again with my fist, for a long time. When it opened, I almost banged Jamelee in the forehead, Bird standing there, holding her close.

"Thank goodness," I gushed. "I didn't know if you could hear me."

I tried to step in, around her, but she brought the door closer to her shoulder.

"I think you'd do best at your mother's awhile."

"What?"

"You heard what I said."

It was like she was going to shut the door on me. I put my hand out to stop it. She looked at it, then me, furious.

"Bird, what's happening?"

"'What's happening?'" She said it nasty. "'What's *happening?*' All I know 'what's happening' is the police are coming to my house, searching my goddamn car, asking me questions about fools I can't stand the sight of. Questioning my *grandmomma.* I know 'what's happening' is you lying to the police and you lying to me, and I don't want it in my house. You go on and stay with your momma. You ain't staying here."

"You know I can't do that." I started to cry a little.

"You do what you have to, but I'm telling you, you ain't doing it here no more."

Jamelee was pulling at Bird's necklaces, and Bird swatted her fat little arm.

"Bird, don't—" I meant the baby then, more than me.

She started to shut the door again.

"At least let me get some of my things." My voice was ugly, pleading. Guilty. I hated the sound of it. "I need my purse."

She stared at me a long cold minute, still blocking the doorway with most of the door and the rest of herself. Finally she walked away, leaving only a dark space where she had been. But at least the door was open.

I walked through the house, to my room, almost like I was blind. The whole morning was unreal. First the police, the search, and now Bird telling me I had to leave. It couldn't be happening. Like none of it had happened—not Saturday, not this, not anything. In my room, I found my old duffel and tried to put some things into it. I couldn't see much because I'd started to cry. It wasn't just going to my momma's that was making me scared. It was Bird, telling me I had to.

And then Bird was in the doorway. Watching me as I stood there, shoulders shaking, the bag stupid in my hand. I knew I had to tell her then so that she would understand—understand that even if they searched her car, she wouldn't be in trouble. I had to reassure her, right now, by telling her the whole thing. I just wasn't sure I knew how to do it in a way that would still protect Dee.

"Bird, let me expla—"

Her fist against the doorframe made me jump.

"There ain't nothing I want to hear from you, you

understand? Ain't nothing you say but a bunch of *lies*. You get out of my house right now and you don't come back. Not until you talking truth, if you even know what that is."

"Bird, I didn't—"

"Get *out* of my house! Get out, I'm telling you! Just get out!"

It was like she was going to push me herself if I didn't move. So crying, snuffling, gasping, shuffling, I went past her, down the hall. The TV was on in the front room. A cop show. It wasn't funny to me in the slightest that on it, someone was getting busted.

I WOKE UP IN MY BED—MY OLD BED, AT CHERRY'S. THE light was on. I didn't know how long I'd been asleep or what time it was, but it was dark outside. I didn't remember much besides walking over there from Bird's, drinking all three beers I found in the fridge, curling up on the bed, and crying, crying, crying.

"What are you doing here?" Cherry said to me from the doorway. She was wearing the black pants and white button-down that meant she'd been at work. Wherever that was this time. Her hair was up, and her lipstick had crusted in a dark line around the edges of her lips. She needed me to retouch her roots.

"I'm staying here for a while."

She looked at me, eyes loose—everything in her loose. Loose

but not so much so that she wouldn't fly into a tightened rage at any moment. My body clenched up. She looked at her nails a minute.

"You'll need to pay rent, then."

I heard how small my voice was when I said, automatic, "But the house is paid for."

She snorted. "Yeah, but my patience with you isn't." Then she disappeared down the dark hall. I could hear her hand sliding down the wall, guiding her a little.

She hadn't turned off the light.

IN THE MORNING, I MADE SURE TO GET UP EARLY. I GOT
dressed, quietly, but I should've known it didn't matter how
much noise I made. Cherry was asleep on the couch, the DVD
still rotating its constant dramatic menu. I took her car keys from
her purse and pulled the door shut, silent as I could. I wouldn't
be gone long. She wouldn't notice. And it would take a lot, most
likely, to wake her.

I didn't know what I was going to say to Dee, really. Didn't
know what I could realistically ask of him, right now. Only knew
that I had to see him. And, no matter what he said, I knew—
from the other night, and always—that he needed me, too. Only
a week had passed, but it seemed like years since last Saturday.
Years since he picked me up from work that Friday, me flushed

faced and excited, picturing a whole romantic weekend of just us. Each day since, almost a lifetime of things had happened. And he was wrong that being apart was the best thing for us right now. If he was too stubborn to know it, I was going to help him remember.

It wasn't a long drive to his gym, but I sped with the rest of traffic anyway. The place was huge, and glossy, the parking lot full of cars. His big black truck towered over them. Hurrying inside, I hoped he was mostly done with his workout. Otherwise he'd be mad I interrupted.

The California-looking guy behind the reception counter gave me a smile but was still curious since it was pretty clear I was no gym regular. I told him I was looking for my boyfriend.

"What's his name?" The guy had a name tag—Steve. "I can page him."

"Oh no. If it's okay, I'll just walk through."

He nodded and smiled again, then went back to his computer. He wasn't interested in me at all, or who I was looking for.

I found Dee upstairs, sitting on a weight bench, talking to a monstrous guy made up of muscley ridges. Dee had a towel around his neck, tattooed hands clenching either end. He was glistening with sweat, and his ribbed tank top clung to his chest. A smile went over me just seeing him. I wanted to be invisible then so I could watch him like this—easy and relaxed, chatting with a friend.

But he must've seen me from the corner of his eye, because he turned and stood up before I even got near.

"What are you doing here?"

Close up, I could smell him—his man smell. Sweat, and more. Strength. I started to cry with relief.

"I just had to talk to you and I didn't know what else."

"You've got to cut this out." He was annoyed at first, mean like he gets. But then, softer, "I need you to be strong."

He took me by the elbow and guided me down the wide stairs, the chrome railings gleaming past us. All I felt was his hand, tight and safe around my elbow. I wanted to sink into the feeling. I didn't care where he was pushing me.

Outside, the heat from the asphalt curled up around our legs. I had to squint to look at him, but my vision was blurred from tears anyway.

"Dee, they came to Bird's house. They searched her—"

"Look, I'm trying to act as normal as I can here, but you're starting to mess all that up. What did I tell you? Just keep your mouth shut and quit freaking out."

"But, Dee, they're going to question her grandma."

"And she's gonna say Bird was with her, and, hell, they'll go to the outlets and see her on their fucking tapes if they need to, and she'll be fine. Why're you worrying about her anyway? You think the cops didn't come to my house too? You think they're not watching me, even when I'm at work?"

"Are you okay?"

He laughed. "They can't do shit to me, baby. They ain't got nothing. I'm telling you, we just got to ride this out. They can fuss all they want. We sit tight, act cool, it'll fizzle out."

"I don't know if I can without you."

I put my arms around his waist and pressed myself as close to him as I could. My head against the hard muscle of his chest. His heart, loud and strong. But he curled himself out of my arms.

"Listen, you can't be coming around like this. To my gym. To my house. We need to take a break. It's better if we don't see each other for a while. And I mean, at all."

"But why? If everything is okay like you say—"

"You don't hear me talking to you?"

I put my hand on his forearm, trying to be calm in spite of how mad he was. "I hear you, Dee, I just don't understand."

He cursed and spit, shook his head, staring at his feet.

I tried again: "Bird made me go to my momma's."

A scowl crawled over his face. "What do you expect me to do about that?"

"I don't know, Dee. I just—I really miss you. I don't think I can—"

"You can and you will." His voice was sharp. Then he sighed, and his hand was back on my arm, rubbing up and down, like I might be cold. "Why did you think I wanted you with me, baby, huh? Because I knew you could do what I needed you to. Whatever I asked."

My eyes went to the place on his chest where his tattoo was. Though it was covered by his tank, I could still see it in my mind. I still needed to know—over and over—that the *N* stood for *Nikki*, and nothing else.

"Are you seeing her, Dee? Is that why?"

"Who?"

"You know who."

His jaw muscles tightened. "How the fuck do you think I could be seeing her right now, Nikki, huh? How do you think I'd be managing that? Hmmm? Genius? I'm not seeing nobody. Including you right now, you understand me? Now get out of here. Don't call me, don't send me any of your whiny texts. Just sit tight, keep quiet, do what you have to do to calm that friend of yours down, and don't say anything else to the cops. I'll tell you if there's anything else to say, and I'll call you when it's cool."

"But, Dee, I can't—"

"You can, baby." He put his arms around me, held me close. He murmured in my ear, breath swirling on my neck, fizzing everything inside me. "You can because we have to. Okay?"

I clung to his back. He let go and stepped away.

"I gotta get in the shower, all right? Go get cleaned up yourself. Take yourself to the movies or something. Forget about Bird. She'll calm down too. There's a lot of fuss right now, but I promise, those pigs can't touch me. Us."

He was walking backward while he talked. I wanted him to tell me he loved me. He hadn't said it in a while, but I knew he wouldn't now. Not from this distance. He liked to say it to me close so that only I could hear.

THAT AFTERNOON, I SLEEPWALKED THROUGH MY SHIFT AT the salon. When I got home, Cherry told me to clean up because she was having friends over. "A welcome home party," she said, sarcastic. I watched as she put out a sorry plate of cheese and grapes and heated up salsa with Velveeta in it. She dumped some tortilla chips into one of Grandma's crystal bowls. I went into the bathroom and stood under the shower for as long as I could.

When I was dressed, three people were already there. Men. They sat around the kitchen table with Cherry, drinking and smoking and talking. I moved around them to get myself a beer and then tried to leave, but they had other ideas.

"Aw, don't go, honey," one of them said. He had long gray

hair and was wearing a puffy down vest and no shirt. "Sit down, tell us about yourself."

"She does hair," Cherry told them, voice dry and flat.

"You think you could do something about this mess?" the skinny, darker man said. I'd seen him before. I thought his name was Leroy. He was rubbing and rubbing the long-haired guy's head, pressing it down all the way to the table. "Fuckin' man's got things *living* in there. You ain't an exterminator too, are you?"

Everyone laughed while Leroy and the guy in the vest fake wrestled a minute. I saw the third guy, much younger than all of them, watching me as I dunked a chip into the microwaved salsa-cheese mess just so I wouldn't have to answer.

Bo came in with Mary and Cecille, and the house got more lively. Cherry made me offer everybody drinks, like this was some kind of proper party. She cackled at nothing while I moved around, making me tell dumb stories she should be telling herself, like about the time I swallowed one of my own loose teeth when I was little. I hated talking, hated her asking me things she knew were embarrassing, hated all of them watching me. But after not very long, she lifted her eyebrows to Bo and stopped paying attention to me. They paraded back into her bedroom to snort. Her and Bo, at first, and then pairs of them every fifteen minutes, sometimes in larger groups. While Cherry was back there, two other women showed up, one of them talking on her phone nonstop, her face scabby though she'd tried to cover it with makeup. I let them in but made them get their own drinks. I took two beers and went to my room.

Not that there was much to do, except get away from all of them. There wasn't any TV, and we'd never had a computer. I didn't have many books, and I hadn't thought to bring any old magazines from the salon today either. I found a pack of cards in the bedside table and sat on my bed, sipping beer and playing Solitaire.

After about an hour there was a knock at my door. When I opened it, Cherry was standing there, giggling.

She crooked her finger at me, beckoning. "You gotta come out here."

"I'm not in the mood."

She laughed, bending forward. "Oh-ho, honey. You will be." She looked down the hall and hollered, "Emilio! Emilio, get your narrow ass over here." To me, she said, "You've made quite an impression, little girl."

Behind her I saw the younger guy step into the hall. He had his hands in his pockets, shy, but his eyes had the same druggy gleam my mother's did.

I shoved past her. "Leave me alone." I pushed past Emilio too, into the living room, where Leroy and Bo and Cecilia were grinding to the music. Behind me Cherry called my name, but I didn't even turn. I just went out through the kitchen, to the back of the house, and into the dark. I walked to the only safe place I knew—to Bird's. I hadn't even been at my momma's for a day, and already it was starting: her selling me off to her friends. I couldn't stay there. I couldn't. But I didn't have anywhere else to go, either. Bird was my only hope. But I didn't know how to make her not mad at me.

I stood at the curb at the edge of her yard, trying to picture myself saying something and knowing there was nothing I could that would make anything right enough for her.

Except, of course, the truth.

ONE HOUR, TWO. I'M NOT SURE HOW LONG I WAS THERE ON
the curb outside Bird's house, trying to get the courage to go
knock on her door. Eventually the lights went out. I didn't want
to wake her or Jamelee up, not for this. As I walked—slow—back
to Cherry's, I told myself the daytime would be better anyway.
She'd be fresher headed, and more time between our fight
would've passed. I sat, numb, on the curb just down the street
from our house until Cherry and her friends piled out the front
door and into Bo's car. They roared past me, not even seeing.
Only then did I let myself in. I went straight to my room and
locked the door.

Sunday I stayed in bed as late as I could, listening for noises
of Cherry coming home that never happened. I thought of Bird,

at church, and later dinner with her grandma. I wanted so bad to be sitting at that table with them, listening to Rose's stories and passing along more biscuits. But Bird wouldn't want me there. So I waited. A shamed little corner of me hoped something about the Lord's day would fill her with more forgiveness, too. Tomorrow. I would talk to her tomorrow.

I could've gone somewhere on the bus, I guess, but I didn't want to leave and then come back with Cherry and her crew around. So I sat on the couch and watched DVDs from her bootlegged collection. As I lay there, every inch of me felt ready to spring up at the sound of Bo's car, rush back into my room, and lock the door. But even after the second movie, no sound came. Sometime around four, I found a box of macaroni and cheese in the pantry and made it for myself, though Cherry had no milk and there was no telling how long the butter had been in there. No beer left to speak of either, and no one around to buy me any. Nothing to do but feel sorry for myself.

By seven o'clock I was bored and bleary eyed from so much TV. I paced the length of the living room a few times, trying to think. Cherry might have money in her bedside table, the pocket of her robe, but I was afraid to go in her room at all. The edge of the doorway was about as far as I went when it came to her space anymore.

All I needed to get me through until tomorrow really was

one little word from Dee. Yesterday had been so off, so wrong. The timing had been all bad, and we both knew it. I just needed one little hit now to make things right again, to get things straight. Just a "Hey, baby," or "I love you"—something sweet from him since he hadn't had a chance to say anything like that yesterday. Gaps between communication were normal, but never when things were this tense. Not when there was so much going wrong. I just needed to know he was all right, that he was thinking of me. That he knew I was going through a lot too and that all I had to do was keep hanging in there a little while longer. To be strong.

It took a while for me to text him, but once I did, I couldn't stop.

NIKKI: D I just need 2 tlk 1 more time

NIKKI: I dont want 2 mk u mad

NIKKI: Its wrd here

NIKKI: Where r u? Can u cm by?

NIKKI: Im scared & alone

NIKKI: D?

After another hour of waiting without any response, I was about to climb the walls. This wasn't like those other times when I was just missing him. I was at my momma's. I'd had to talk to the police. Bird wasn't speaking to me. He *knew* how bad things were. So why wouldn't he even send me one little hey? The only explanation was that his phone had lost its charge. Or, more likely, something bad had happened. Something awful. I yanked open drawers and cabinets, looking around for a phone book, wishing I could call his house. Even if Cherry had one, though, I still didn't know his father's first name. So after another ten minutes, I dialed Dee's phone.

Before it rang even half a time, he was shouting in my ear. "Goddamn you."

"Dee—"

"God, God, God, God, God, God *damn* you. You can't do a single goddamn thing I tell you, can you, huh? Not one single thing. 'We need a break for a while, Nikki,' I say to you, and here you are, texting me fifty times, crying, messing everything up."

I hadn't been crying before. But now I was.

"Dee, I'm sorry, but I'm here at my momma's and there's no one, and I can't go anywhere and I'm scared and I need you—"

"'I need you,'" he fake whined. "You thinking at all about what I need, Nikki? Huh? You thinking about that? While you're sitting in your momma's pretty house, no one caring where you are or what you do?"

I wiped my face. Hearing him, even if he was mad, was better than not. "Of course I am. That's why I called—I was so worried."

"I don't think so. I think all you're thinking about, all you ever stinking think about, is your fat self and what can I do to pull you up. What you can get out of me."

"You know I'll do anything for you, Dee, I just—"

He chuckled, low. "Yeah, well, what I really need is to just get the hell out of here for a while."

"Anywhere, Dee. Anywhere. I have some money. It's not much, but it might last a little bit. We could get into South Carolina, maybe go to the beach."

Another laugh, this one meaner. "I ain't taking you nowhere no more."

"I don't . . . understand."

"Understand this, you hear me? I. Never. Want to see. Your face. Again. I'm changing my phone number, so help me God, if you try to call it one more time. You hear me, Nikki? I'm getting out of here, and if you so much as send me one tiny text or do anything else to mess up what I been trying to take care of, I swear to sweet Mary, mother of Jesus, that I will smash this phone so deep into your skull that it'll print on the back side of your brain. You get me? Or do you need me to spell it out?"

I was shaking. He was mad, scared, sure. Just like me. But it was because of everything going on. We just needed to calm down. This was what happened when we couldn't press our bodies close.

"Dee, I—"

"Do not. Call me. Again. You understand? And don't think of saying anything to anyone else. You fucked it up. You fucked everything up. Now leave me alone, keep your mouth shut, and just don't fuck it up even more."

"Don't, Dee, please. I swear, I'm sorry—"

But then he was gone.

I WOKE UP WITH MY CLOTHES STILL ON, THE LIGHT BY MY bedside burning. My phone was still in my hand, pressed up under my stomach. I'd fallen asleep hoping Dee would call back, tell me how sorry he was, but it never rang and everything was blank. Dee was gone. I didn't know where, and I didn't know when he was coming back. How long it would take him to cool off this time. It was morning, early. Seven thirty. I tiptoed to my door and opened it a crack, looking down the hall to Cherry's room. But the door was wide open and no one was inside. She and Bo still bingeing, I guess. But it wasn't going to be long before she needed money again. I wondered, now that I was eighteen, if I'd be as valuable to her as before.

I showered quickly and got ready for work, where I had to

be at eleven. Plenty of time to talk to Bird, get it all worked out. After what Dee said last night—even if he didn't really mean it—I needed her now even more than ever. I had to have someone around me who could at least partly understand, who could help me get through without him for a while.

Outside, it was warm and muggy, so sweat beaded immediately on my lip as I walked down to Bird's, stood on her step. I listened to the sounds of the TV inside, trying to get the nerve to knock. I was going to tell her everything. Everything. But I couldn't be sure if she was alone in there right now or not. Kenyetta lived close enough to walk over, and so did Bird's cousin, along with several other folks Bird did regular sewing jobs for. Anybody else could be in there, even this early, and I didn't want company.

The final thing that made me knock was thinking if someone else was here, maybe it would keep Bird from getting really angry.

Her face in the little window of the front door clouded as soon as she pulled back the curtain and saw me. She shook her head and tried to say something.

"Bird, please," I said, loud. "I need to talk to you."

She looked into the room behind her and said something else. Then she faced me and shook her head again.

"Bird, I really need to talk. About everything. The truth, I swear."

She dropped the curtain down. Another wait, and finally the front door came open. But it wasn't Bird. It was Kenyetta. She exploded out of the house, into my face, pushing me back down the steps before I even knew what was happening. "Oh, no you don't!" she yelled, her long, hard nails scraping against my shoulders and chest as she shoved. "Oh no-ho, you don't. Bird got too good a soul to call the police on your sorry ass this minute, but I don't got *no* trouble doing just that. She don't want to hear nothing you got to say anymore now, you hear me?" I was stepping back, but she kept coming at me, finger pointing. "You so stupid, telling her ain't nothing else going to happen, thinking the police will just come take a glance at her car and then leave her alone like they's nothing else. Like they won't slap her with charges if they find one *scrap* of anything connected to that boy. Like this ain't the beginning of just a whole world of trouble. They could take her baby, bitch. You ever think about that? They could ask Meelee's daddy, did he give up his custody legal. It happened to my cousin. Bird could be in court for the rest of her life. She won't say it—she too good—but I can, and I say you the most low-down, selfish, no-good whore I ever seen. You get out of here and don't you *never* let me see your face. Not in this yard, not on that step, not even on this street, or so help me I'll make you sorry you even *looked* at that nasty-ass, cop-killing gangbanger you fooling with."

Bird had come out onto the front step and was watching us. "That's enough, Yetta," she said, tired but calm. "We don't know any of that's going to happen."

Kenyetta whipped back around to glare at me. "I do. I know. From more than one example." Her hands were on her hips, but she looked like she might lunge at me again. "My sister's ex-husband had this man working for him in his air-condition business. Man got busted for weed or some such and the police were all *over* that office, looking at papers, hiring records, and all that. He had to pay some big-ass fine just not to go to jail himself. Those police don't mess around, girl. It ain't like you just say, 'Oh, but, Officer, I'm a good person,' and they leave you be."

I didn't know if what Kenyetta was saying was true, but even if she was lying about her ex-brother-in-law and her cousin, something cold in me knew it would end up being true about this, about Bird.

"Bird, I just wanted to talk to you," I said over Kenyetta's shoulder. If she would just listen, just hear me out and let me explain, I knew we would figure out a solution. We would get out of this mess.

"She don't want to talk to you, whore-ass trouble," Kenyetta muttered.

Bird wasn't looking at either me or Kenyetta but somewhere else, far off.

"Bird, please."

"You get out of here," Kenyetta said. I kept watching Bird, begging her with my eyes, my thoughts, my heart, to please just talk to me. But she wouldn't. She told Kenyetta to come on and went inside without looking my way.

I WALKED BACK TO CHERRY'S TO GET MY PURSE. SHE STILL wasn't there, but I didn't leave a note. Mostly because, for the first time in a long time, I wasn't thinking of anyone else but Bird. Bird and what Kenyetta had said, about them maybe being able to take Jamelee away. I couldn't let that happen. Not after everything Bird had done for me. I knew at least that much. But it was like I didn't know anything else. Not then, and not while I was sitting on the bus, or during the long, hot walk. I wasn't thinking, and I wasn't crying either. I just was. Like a sleepwalker. Or like someone who has accepted a thing that she knew all along Fate was going to wind up making her do, and now it was time to do it.

I pulled the glass door open. It was dim inside. I told them, "I need to talk to Detective DuPree."

IT TOOK A WHILE FOR THE DETECTIVE TO SEE ME, BUT WHEN he did, it wasn't just him. Like he knew I was going to have something important to say. He took my name, my age, and asked me a few questions to determine whether I was crazy or on drugs, and then I started the story. They began writing at once, all three of them. During this, a part of me was there, in the room, telling them what they needed to know, but another part of me was reliving the whole thing in more detail than I'd remembered before. Much more than I was actually saying out loud.

Dee picked me up from work at four thirty on Friday. He doesn't do that often, and the other girls all looked at me with knowing, jealous pride. My man. Coming to take me out on a Friday. I waved to them and giggled. They clucked behind me. Dee and I drove to get beer and then the drive-through at Checkers to get dinner. Food for Bird too.

Of course the beer part I didn't say. Or even about the girls at the salon. Just the time he picked me up, and that we'd gotten food, went to Bird's. It felt important to tell them those things since, for me, it was when the whole weekend started.

Dee had weed, so we all smoked up—even Bird a little—all of us chilling, watching TV. The baby rolling on the floor. Laughing. Us all getting silly. Eventually the baby went down to bed and we played this drinking game Dee knows called the Pope Is Russian before we all went to sleep ourselves.

My mouth knew to skip over these things, though my mind didn't.

The next morning, he was on me before I was even awake. Hungry. Needing. Full of love. He finished and we went into the kitchen and I made biscuits. I felt happy, calm. It had been so nice that Bird and Dee got along the night before, that he was in such a good mood. We ate together, tired and bleary but laughing. Dee went to the gym and Bird and I cleaned up, got Jamelee ready so they could go out shopping with Bird's grandma Rose and auntie Melora. I gave the baby a bath so that Bird got some time on her own. And I let myself get a little dressed up too, thinking about what Dee and I might do together, by ourselves.

When Ms. Rose and Melora came to get Bird, I saw Dee pulling

*up along the curb too. I expected him to come in, but he didn't. Just
Bird's auntie and grandma, without knocking. They stood in the
kitchen telling me I should come with them, but I said I was having
a special weekend with my boyfriend instead. I saw Melora give Bird
a look, but Ms. Rose shook her finger at me in a sly way and laughed.
Dee finally got out of his truck as we all came out of the house. He
had some kind of overnight bag in his hand, which I know he didn't
have when he left. It wasn't the same thing he put his gym clothes in,
either. I wondered if we were going to a hotel somewhere.*

*Bird and them all said hello to him, polite, but he didn't smile
much back. As they drove off, Ms. Rose hollered out the window to
Dee, "You take her somewhere nice." He lifted his hand, watching
them. I was glad I'd had time to put on one of my cute tops and
made sure there were plenty of condoms around. As I stood next to
Dee in the driveway, everything felt very . . . special.*

I didn't say nearly all of that either. Mostly just that Dee got
back from the gym as Bird was leaving. That I knew they'd be
away all day.

*As soon as they were gone, he asked me did I have those wigs he
asked me for before.*

*"We going to a costume party?" I was feeling light and sassy. But
he just scowled, so I told him they were in the closet.*

*I'd ordered the two wigs, special, from the salon weeks ago: one
short brown—almost like a man's—and the other a long flowing red*

one. I didn't know why he needed them. These exact styles. All he'd said when I asked was, "I gotta do something."

I brought them to him. He nodded and took them off their foam heads. He stuffed them into his bag, which I could see had clothes in it, most of them black.

I asked him what was up.

"It's a surprise." He kind of smiled. "Let's go."

I asked him where we were going.

"Just on a drive."

When I locked the door behind us, I saw him looking at Bird's car.

"How long's Bird gone?" he wanted to know.

"Probably all day," I told him. I put my arms around his waist and rubbed my face between his shoulder blades. Let my hands move down toward his belt buckle. I wanted to go back in the house, restart what we had going on this morning.

"Let's take her car, then," he said.

I thought he was right, Bird's car would be more exciting, but that we should check with her first. Maybe on this occasion, since it was special, she'd be okay with it.

He put his hand on my wrist as I reached for my phone.

"Baby, you know she don't like me." He was smiling down at me. Sexy. Winking.

I told him okay, but we had to get her some gas while we were out.

I skipped over the parts about the wigs and the clothes to

the police. I didn't want them to know he'd been planning it, thinking ahead. But everything about Bird's Mustang I made sure to say all of. So they understood Bird had no idea we'd taken her car, didn't know anything about it.

We got in, and Dee put the bag at his feet. We held hands, sweet. He told me to head to the interstate. Dee put the stereo on, loud, but the pulsing music felt good. A kind of holiday, just the two of us.

I didn't pay much attention to what we passed or even, really, how long I was driving. It just felt good, letting Dee lead me wherever he wanted. A surprise. Eventually he told me to get off the interstate, and we drove some more, turned, drove, turned. I didn't really know where we were, but there were brand-new strip malls and steak houses and the biggest Walmart I've ever seen. Eventually he told me to slow down, turn into a subdivision. There was a brick sign at the entrance, the name in cursive. The houses were bigger and newer and farther apart than the ones in our neighborhood. We took another turn and he told me to stop the car just past this yellow house with a pretty front porch. Full of plants. I had no idea who lived there. I thought maybe it was a party, though there weren't many other cars around. Was I finally going to meet his family? His friends? Again, I was glad I'd gotten a little dressed up.

He looked out my window. "You see down there?"

He was pointing slightly behind us, between two other houses. I don't remember what they looked like, but the grass between them was bright and damp. I thought, for a second, I wanted to lie down in it with Dee.

He told me to follow the road we were on all the way to the stop sign, go through it, and then take the very first left into a cul-de-sac that ended on the other side of those two houses.

"When I tell you," he said, "you drive over there, and I'll meet you."

I was starting to get a strange feeling. I asked him what he was going to do.

"Don't you trust me?" he said.

"Yes, of course," I said right back.

He took out the short brown wig and handed it to me. That, and a big, mildew-smelling flannel shirt. "Then put these on."

I was trying to keep the idea in my head that this was some kind of funny game—maybe some elaborate trick to play on his mom or something—but I didn't like the creepy way it was feeling. When I asked him about it again, though, he got mad.

"Just put it on and shut up," he said.

So I put on the wig and watched him as he pulled a billowy ladies' blouse out of the bag and took off his T-shirt. He put on the blouse. For a strange reason I wanted to laugh, but the serious look on his face, and the way he kept looking around at the other houses, it wasn't funny at all. He took out a black miniskirt and put that on too. Tights. His boots back on over those. I knew then something was really wrong.

But when I told him I wanted to leave, he got angry. Yelling things like "shut the fuck up," and "keep your ugly mouth shut," and "you'll do what I fucking tell you to do." Everything around me got sharp and bright. I was blinking, fast, feeling really scared but not knowing what to do. My heart was racing. This was no romantic getaway.

I paused. Those disguises—I'd skipped over them in my story, but it made me feel the same strangeness thinking of them again. How intentional it all seemed. But then I took a breath and remembered my purpose. All I needed to do was give them enough to keep them away from Bird. Just to tell them we were there, but not her. At the scene. I told them Dee was acting strange, and I was scared. I couldn't help that part because it was so true.

He put the wig on and reached into the bag again. Two guns. I started freaking out. He grabbed my wrist, squeezing hard. I thought he might punch me, but he didn't. Instead he leaned in, kissed me hard.

"I gotta do something," he told me. And it was hypnotizing, how sure and calm he was. "I need you to be cool. I need you to help me do this. Just this one thing. Don't ask me any more questions, all right? Just do what I tell you. When I say, drive past the stop sign, and turn into the cul-de-sac, and wait for me there. That's all you have to do."

I asked him was he robbing somebody. Was this for his gang. He put his hand over my mouth, and I could see his eyes, wide and deep. For a minute I couldn't see anything else.

"I need you, baby," he said.

My pulse was pounding in my neck, but his hand on my mouth, the pressure of his eyes on me, made everything less crazy. A car came down the road behind us. I saw it in the rearview, and I guess I was still freaked out a little bit because for a minute I thought it was going to ram us from behind. I wanted to get out of there, get me and Dee away, and I started the car, which made Dee start cussing again, but then the car behind us started slowly backing into the driveway. In front of the yellow house.

Dee told me to get ready and gripped the guns tight up against his chest.

He wouldn't look at me anymore. He put his hand on the door handle. Through the window I could see the car in the driveway come to a stop.

Dee said, "Go now. Go, go, drive," and at the same time he was somehow out, slamming the door shut. This all happened in about two seconds. I watched him cross the street. Four strides, five, and then up the driveway, aiming the guns out straight. I heard the shots, loud and fast, and my foot just automatically went down hard on the gas pedal because I didn't want to see what was happening. Bird's Mustang lunged down the road, pulling me with it. For a minute I didn't know what to do with the wheel and was afraid I was going to crash. *The shots kept coming. It was like they were following me. I could barely stay on the road.*

The turn for the cul-de-sac came up quick, and I almost missed it. I thought I might've hit a mailbox. I was blinking, blinking so hard. Like I couldn't see. The second I stopped where Dee told me, he came running from between the houses, just like he said. His long red wig-hair was flying, and I remember thinking, "He looks like a god." Like he was some kind of angry majestic Mexican god of fire or war. And then the driver's side door yanked open and he was pushing me across the seat, bruising me, banging my knee on the shift, shoving me into the passenger's side. The car jolted forward again as he started driving, and he threw the guns in my lap, told me to put them in the glove compartment. He was breathing hard and I knew not to ask him what had happened. I knew what happened. And I didn't want to know at all.

We hauled out of the subdivision, and were back on the interstate in no time. I was shaking, breathing ragged, so stunned I couldn't scream or cry or say anything. His bag was at my feet, a gaping hole of black. I felt the heat of the guns in my lap, and I had to get them off me. I knew enough, though, even in all of it, to hold them with the edge of the smelly flannel shirt so I wouldn't leave any print behind. I slammed the compartment door shut, but it felt like they were sitting there, steaming, watching me.

Finally I could talk. I asked Dee what the hell just happened.

I barely told them any of this. Definitely not about Dee's guns. Only that a car came up behind us, Dee got out, I heard gunshots, freaked out, and drove away. I told them Dee caught up with me around the corner, out of breath, and we left. I told them he didn't say much to me and that we just drove. Because in reality I'd screamed, "What did you just do?" and he answered me in a crazy, too-guilty sounding way. Right now for them, and Bird, I just needed to get the record straight. But I didn't have to tell them exact.

He didn't answer right off. And for that minute, I thought he was going to blow up at me. But then I looked over at him, and he was smiling. This big, beautiful, happy smile. He grinned like that and slapped his hand down on my thigh, started hollering, "We did it, baby!" and, "Woo-hooo, we fucking did it!" Like he just won the lottery and couldn't believe it. He kept laughing, ripping the red wig off and throwing it at my feet, saying, "Oh my God," and, "We did it right on." I couldn't believe how happy he was.

I asked who he'd shot. I was still shaking, but seeing him so excited made me shake less. He told me it was just somebody who got what he deserved. A thing that needed to be done.

"I thought you were going to freak," he said, leaning over to kiss me on the side of the face. "Asking those questions, bugging out, but man, it was perfect." He slammed his hand on the steering wheel, giddy, narrating how he got out of the car, just walked up to him and

then *BLAM BLAM.* He held his fingers into gun shapes. He would not stop grinning. He looked at me, so proud.

"And you. Fuckin' Ciree can't even drive like you sometimes, babe, I swear."

I couldn't help smiling too then. His happiness was like something you could catch. Beside him, I felt all the fear fizzling. I told him how crazy he seemed, running between those houses.

"Baby, I was crazy!" he screamed, raising himself off the seat and shrieking at the windshield, face full of victory. "Totally fucking crazy, man."

He laughed like a kid. A kid being tickled so bad he might wet his pants. It was scary, and terrible, and . . . awesome. I thought of the other girl then, his old girlfriend. The one he came back to me from—and no wonder. I knew she had never seen him like this, this wild. Or if she had, it had made her too afraid. She would have thought he was a monster. Nobody else could see and understand and love this part of him. This, I knew, was all for me.

His hand squeezed my thigh, kneading, moving higher and higher, up to the curved place just before the bottom of my fly.

"I got an idea," he said, smiling that wild smile.

Before long we were in the far-right lane, blinker clicking. The tight, quiet sound of Bird's car was a cocoon around us. We exited into a rest stop, and his hand pressed harder. I felt my eyelids flutter briefly shut.

He found a parking space, back by picnic tables too far away for any families to want to use. We were in the shade, under a big tree, far away from all the other cars. At the other side of the lot, there were fat ladies in zip-up suits climbing out of vans to walk their tiny dogs and men hitching up their belts on their way to the bathrooms, but nobody could see us.

Dee murmured in my ear, his tongue flicking. "We did it," he said, leaning in to my neck and pressing his hand between my thighs. "You didn't fuck up."

I put my arms around his neck, pressed him closer to me. He was electric, and I wanted to feel his buzz all the way to my bones. His hands started roving, mouth on me all at once, and I didn't want to wait. I climbed over into the backseat, lay myself down, already undoing my jeans. I thought he was a god over me, full of power. And I knew I was the only place he had to put all his energy. I knew, so clearly, that I was the only one who could take it all in, who could open up and give him what he needed.

I didn't say it like that, though.

"We drove straight back to Bird's," was all I told them. "And you know the rest from my statement before."

While they finished writing, I could feel their judgment on me, their quick-glancing eyes saying, *Why didn't you call the police right away? Why did you wait so long to say something?* But in remembering, and in telling them what they needed to know, that golden feeling I'd had with Dee came back over me—the feeling of being a kind of temple for him. I was someone who worshipped him and understood him, in all the ways he needed and deserved. I could feel them hating me, thinking I was wrong, but they'd never had Dee's hands on them, never felt him as completely as I had.

They could judge me all they wanted. But they would never understand.

AFTER THAT, EVERYTHING MOVED VERY FAST. I TOLD THEM
what they needed, they wrote it down, and then suddenly the
young policeman was standing up and saying, "Nicola Rachelle
Dougherty, you are under arrest for being party to the murder of
Deputy Duane Palmer. You have the right to remain silent. . . ."

I was stunned. For one, it was strange to hear that cops really
did that part. The whole thing, just like on TV. About can and
will be held against you. Given a lawyer if you can't afford one.
But more shocking than that was that they were arresting me at
all. I didn't know they could, didn't think they might. It hadn't
been in my head at all when I went to the station this morning.
All I wanted was to get them away from Bird. But now they were
putting handcuffs on me. It was really happening, and I couldn't

believe any of it, real as all the details around me felt. There was a hand gripping me above my elbow, guiding me down a hall. A cold hard office chair. Waiting for hours for someone to process my papers. Cinder block everywhere. Picture taken. Fingerprints. STD test. Thick strong bodies moving around me. Another long hallway. Facing too many people—mean and bored—inside the drunk tank, and more waiting. A door clanging shut. Just like TV. And just like TV, it was like watching it happen to someone else.

Except it really was me.

HOURS. MORE HOURS AND HOURS OF WAITING. IT WAS impossible to tell how long it was, because every minute took forever. I stared at the floor mostly, trying not to see the things behind my eyes, but not wanting to look around either. At people sitting there or leaning against the wall. Some of them talking about what they were in for. Some of them saying this was bullshit. Some of them not the kind of people you'd expect to see in a place like this at all. Some exactly what you'd imagine. Every now and then, one of them getting called out because someone had posted their bail.

All I could think, even though I knew it was foolish, was that I hoped I'd get to make my phone call before they got to Dee. I hoped he really had gotten out of town. I imagined the sound of his voice when he answered, what I might say. What words of strength he might give to me: *I'll wait for you, you'll wait for me. It'll be okay.* It wasn't like I wanted to warn him. Only to tell him that I was sorry and that though I hadn't told them much, I hadn't had any choice about what I did say. When they finally came to get me, I pressed the numbers slow, my throat clenched around tears. But his phone went straight to voice mail.

"Dee." I tried not to shake, knowing this might be my last chance to explain. But it was hard to talk, thinking I would probably never hear from him again. And he might not even listen to the message. "I love you so much. I love you so much still, and I will always. I'm so sorry, but I had to. I didn't have a choice. But I love you, baby, and I miss you and I'm so sorry."

There wasn't anything else to say. Especially not with an officer standing there, watching me.

"No lawyer, huh?" she said after I hung up.

I shook my head.

"Didn't think so."

She led me down another hall to a lobby where three other people I'd been in the drunk tank with were sitting. Hands on knees, heads down. She told everyone to stand up, follow her, because it was time to ride over to the jail. Two other officers walked behind us as we moved in a line behind her. There was a gray door, beyond which I could hear an engine running. She told us to line up against the wall and then took the first woman through. The rest of us waited, even the officers seeming a little bored and tired.

Standing there in that ugly hallway, tired and scared, it hit me that nobody knew where I was—not Bird, not Dee, not even Cherry. I was going to jail, and for the first time in my life, I was going to be totally, utterly alone.

STRIP SEARCHED.

Yes, I had to bend over and—

Then a shower. No door on the stall, two officers watching.

Another search. It would've been funny to say to Bird, *What did they think I'd hide in there, the cheap-ass soap?* but I wasn't sure anything would be funny again.

The jumpsuit they gave me was orange and scratchy. White T-shirt. A sports bra. Grandma underwear. Flip-flops with thin soles that were hard to keep on my feet while I walked. I didn't know where they took my other clothes.

Handcuffed. This time with a chain around my waist too. And cuffs around my ankles.

Shuffling, following.

The key in the lock. Two beds—the shadow of someone else in the lower one. I realized it was late, though I didn't know what time it was. Guards telling the woman in the bed—I didn't try to see her face—that she had company. Me, climbing up, curling in the middle of the top bunk. The cell door slamming. The woman saying sleepily that her name was Priscilla, and wake up was six a.m. I guess I told her my name too. But mostly I was too scared to move. Or even cry.

IT WASN'T SLEEP, EXACTLY. MORE A NUMBING CLOUD OF shock, enfolded in memories and half dreams and awake thoughts all shifting places with each other until the lights were on and the guards were calling everyone to wake up. I blinked at the ceiling, listening, expecting them to be mean and yelling. Surprised that they weren't. There were just loud calls of, "Good morning, ladies," and, "Time to wake up," and noises of groaning, coming-to-life people. Prisoners. And I was one of them.

"Six a.m., every morning including Sunday," Priscilla said from the bunk underneath me. "Clean up the bunk, then breakfast," she went on. "Better get moving."

I sat up and looked over the edge of my narrow bed. All I could see below me were her knees in orange pants like mine, and her wrists and hands dangling over those. In the curve between her thumb and index finger on her right hand, she had a tattoo—cursive writing of some kind—though I couldn't read it from up here.

"You showing her the ropes, LaSalle?" a heavyset blond guy in scrubs said outside our bars. He was leaning over one of those carts you see maids with in hotels.

"I got it, Archie," she told him.

"Better get moving, then. Breakfast's in twenty."

He slid open the cell door, and Priscilla stood up to take the rags and small bucket of ammonia-smelling water he was handing to her. She moved like you would imagine a boxer would move, and she had the same Mexican bronze skin as Dee. His skin I would maybe never touch again, never feel against my—

My stomach cramped. Priscilla was waving to the guy with the cart and turning back into the cell, her features calm. How could anyone be normal in here? Act like things were fine? Her long jet-black hair was thick and wavy, matted some in the back but basically the kind of hair you didn't have to do a thing to—hardly even wash—for it to be beautiful. It was surprising someone so pretty could ever be in jail.

"Come on, Dougherty," the guy outside—Archie—called to me before he moved on. "I know it's your first day, but you might as well get used to it."

I was amazed he knew my name, let alone that this was my first morning. When he'd wheeled down to the next cell, Priscilla started talking again.

"Archie's okay," she said. "Little too friendly for my taste, chatty I mean, but his wife's been in the hospital and I think he's just lonely and scared."

I nodded, not sure what to say, and stepped down to the first rung of the two-rung ladder between my bunk and hers. I followed what Priscilla was doing and pulled the bottom sheet of my bunk straight, stretched the blanket over that as best I could. I pounded the pillow twice with my fist, knowing that no amount of pounding was going to ever make that pillow fluffy. Not fluffy enough to make me forget Dee's head wasn't on another one, next to mine. I thought of my bed at Cherry's house, with five pillows and a down blanket as thick as my bicep. A bed I had thought before was cold and unkind.

Priscilla reached over my head. "Doesn't make sense to have a sloppy place," she said, pulling things military straight in just a few seconds. "Not a lot of space here. Need to keep it nice. Here—" She handed me the small plastic bucket and a clean but worn-thin rag. "Tuesdays and Thursdays, I just give things a general wipe down—walls, the floor. Toilet, of course."

I looked over at the shiny metal pot in the corner opposite our beds. There was a narrow table that served as a desk, with a row of books along the back, and this provided a small amount of shield between the toilet and the open bars of our cell, but I still couldn't picture myself using it, even with my morning urge to pee coming on. I just couldn't do it—not with someone else so close in here. I went ahead and wiped it down before she could even ask me, though. Gary had told me a long time ago that the best way to make it inside was to be accommodating, but not scared. Confident, but not cocky. At the time I'd thought, *Some kind of life lessons to give your stepdaughter,* but now I was scrambling to remember anything else he told me.

We got the cell in good enough shape, I guess, before it was time for breakfast, though I still hadn't finished with my half of the floor when Archie came back with his cart, collecting our rags and buckets.

"The grits are just as nasty as they look," Priscilla murmured behind me as we moved down the hall in line behind the others. "And at lunch, make sure to get pickles if they have them. May be the only vegetable you see for a while."

The cafeteria was like a cafeteria at school, for the most part: a line where you got your food spooned onto a divided plastic tray and then lines of picnic-style tables, with benches bolted to the floor instead of chairs. Every eight feet or so a guard stood, watching everyone. But just like a school cafeteria, the place was full of chatter. Our block, Priscilla told me, was all girls between the ages of eighteen and twenty-five, and it definitely sounded like it. Black girls and Asian girls and Latino girls and white girls, fat girls and skinny girls, girls with tattoos and scars, girls with skin smooth as a makeup ad. All of them—or enough of them, at least—talking together. Gossiping about boyfriends and family, what was on TV yesterday, who'd been visited by who. I don't know what I'd expected—fighting and meanness, like in the movies. I didn't know whether to be glad and relieved by how regular things seemed or to feel even more horrified. Was I going to get so used to being in jail that it became a social hour for me too? So much so that I'd forget dinners at Bird's, with Jamelee? That I would forget Dee?

Dee. I pictured him as I tried to cut the cardboard-tasting hash browns with the edge of my plastic spoon—the only utensil they gave us. Where was he now? Had he really made it out of the state? Or had they found him anyway because of what I'd said? I didn't want to be here—didn't want any of this to have happened—and I certainly didn't want to be in jail while Dee ran around free. At the same time I knew, if they caught him, it would be much worse for him. And I didn't want that either. I really didn't.

An unexpected wave of anger took over me then. Toward Bird. For making me leave her house and for making me tell. For never, never once giving Dee a chance. At first it felt strange to blame Bird, but the more I thought about her, the righter it became. She was always so convinced she was the only one who knew anything. She never even tried to understand. When she got high and mighty, there wasn't even a shred of kindness or mercy in her. It was her way and her way only, and it made a person feel more than small. Worthless underneath her judgment. Her bossiness. Her needing to do things so holy. If Bird had just left things alone, trusted me even a little, none of this would have happened. It would've blown over, like Dee said. It didn't have to be any of her business. But she had to be the boss of everything, had to make everyone hold to her strict standards. She could never accept anyone for just what they were. She could never really just let me be me. With her, I always had to be more than that. I couldn't just exist, the way I did with Dee. Instead I always had to be the me *she* wanted. The one who fit her requirements. And she'd push me toward it over and over, no matter how clear it was to both of us that I was always going to be too weak and too stupid to come anywhere close to being like her.

The guards called for cleanup, and breakfast was over. I hadn't talked to anyone, though I was aware of Priscilla trying to include me a little in her conversation with the other girls at our table. As they stood up around me, getting ready for whatever was next, I looked at my plate.

My hash browns were severed into tiny bits.

THEY DON'T TELL YOU THAT JAIL IS BORING. ALL MORNING after breakfast I was on edge, watching, afraid something was going to happen. That someone would pick on me or there'd be some kind of trouble. But all that happened was we got taken into the common area, and right away five or six girls started in on some card game tournament. Four other girls parked in front of the TV, two of them taking turns with the remote every hour, in some kind of system. It was annoying shows, and the girls controlling the remote mostly talked to the TV the whole time, but nobody else said anything about it, so I didn't either. Priscilla was reading a book most of the morning, until she got a visitor and came back with four days' worth of crossword puzzles from the paper. She sat there with her pencil and her glasses, looking more like some kind of nerd college kid than a woman in jail.

I tried to read too. Some beat-up romance paperback. But almost every page made me think of Dee, and eventually I pressed my head on the table and my thighs together, trembling with want. How—how?—was I going to get through day after day without him if I could barely make it an hour?

Lunch was worse than breakfast. Priscilla had been right about pickles being almost the only vegetable, besides some sorry too-old lettuce if you dared a baloney sandwich. I struggled with some soup that had a few bits of chicken floating in it, but that made me think of making soup for Bird and Jamelee and eventually I shoved it away. I was both hungry and not. We'd be given commissary rights tomorrow, where you could get some better food. But I didn't have any money. Not more than the maybe fifteen dollars I'd had in my purse when I came in. And I wasn't sure they were going to credit me that anyway. If they did, I was going to need a few sundries before I even thought about chips. But I didn't know if I'd be able to eat those either.

A couple of hours after lunch, one of the guards hollered, "Dougherty," over by the main desk and the phone. "Lawyer here to see you."

Lawyer. I'd forgotten that I'd get one. But then suddenly it was frustrating they'd taken so long to get me one. That I'd had to sleep here first.

A series of buzzes and lights and I was led down another hall into a side room with little in it but a table and two chairs. A youngish guy in a too-big suit stood in front of one of them. A briefcase was on the table.

"Miss Dougherty," he said, all official. He nodded to the guard, and she left the room, standing outside but watching through the glass window in the door.

"Hello, Nikki," he said to me when the door was shut.

I didn't know what else to say but hello.

"Have a seat, please. I'm Doug Jacobsen. They've appointed me as your lawyer."

I sat, waiting for him to keep talking.

"They treating you all right? You doing okay?"

I shrugged. How was I supposed to answer? They were treating me all right. But I would never be okay.

He smoothed his hands over the top of his briefcase before opening it and taking out a folder. "Well, Nikki— please call me Doug—since you cannot provide your own legal counsel, the court has appointed me to represent you." I waited for him to go on. I didn't know what I was supposed to do—what I could do. But it seemed like he wanted me to say something first.

"I've reviewed your case," he said after a long pause. "What's here, at least, and I have to tell you that the charges against you are pretty serious. You do understand that you have, by this statement, essentially confessed to being party to murder? Of a county deputy? Which means they are essentially *charging* you with murder."

"But I didn't kill anybody."

He looked at me. I looked at him back.

"I know that," he finally said. "But with this confession that you made—if I'm correct, voluntarily—it may be difficult, to say the least, to arrange a case that will result in less than—"

"I didn't shoot anybody." I could hear the little girl sound of my voice, but it was the truth. "I just drove. I didn't even really see what happened."

"So, were you forced against your will to drive?"

Forced. Against my will. Was I? Of course not. All of this was too crazy. I didn't know what I was supposed to say, what I felt. We were together, and I was happy, and we went on a drive. And then it was scary and he was wild. There was shooting, and then we were together again. He promised all I had to do was hang on. And now this.

The lawyer's hands spread toward me on the table, reaching. Maybe offering something. I didn't know.

"Let me say this a different way. Are you telling me that you felt coerced into what was happening that day? Did he hit you? Threaten you? If Mr. Pavon *forced* you into this situation, we might—"

I thought. I tried to picture. But mostly I remembered Dee's face in my neck, after. How proud he was. Of himself. And me.

"I was scared, but he didn't . . ." His hand squeezing my arm. His face in my face. But he hadn't *made* me do anything. So did that mean I was guilty? Just because I didn't go straight to the police? And instead went wherever Dee said, did what he told me. Willingly. Happily. Wantingly.

"I just didn't know." I heard my voice collapse. "I didn't know any of what he was going to do."

"All right." Doug was nodding, slow, like I'd made some kind of suggestion and he was accepting it. "Well, we'll do our best here. I still need to review all the evidence against you. But if anything comes to mind—anything at all—that you feel I need to know about that day or about what you told the police, you can call me at any time. The guards know that. In the meantime, your arraignment's been set for Thursday. You'll be brought to the courthouse, you'll make your plea, and your bail will be reset. I'll be there, of course. But because of what you've said to the police, if I were you, I'd go ahead and plead guilty."

I couldn't believe what he was saying.

"I didn't *kill* anyone," I told him again. This wasn't happening. This couldn't happen. Jail even one day was awful. Being without

Dee—probably forever—was a torture I could barely face. But a murder charge? Guilty? Then I might as well not even live. Not when I had not one single person left to turn to. Not a single one.

"How can you ask me to tell a court that I did when I didn't?" I cried. "I'm telling you I didn't do anything!"

My fists were against the table. I was sweating, though the room had a chill.

His face softened for just a moment. "I really think it would be the easier route, Nikki. It'll most likely result in a lesser sentence. And you won't have to go to trial. Trial would be, believe me, an even bigger mess."

"But I can't plead guilty when I didn't *do* anything. I drove where he said. That's all I did. I didn't even drive us home. I didn't know what he was going to do. I didn't even see much of anything. I didn't know any of this. I just wanted to—"

He got sterner. "But you did drive there, and you didn't try to stop him or get away yourself. You helped him leave the scene. And you lied to the police about it. It's all right here. It took you over a week to come forward about what really happened, and in my opinion, you're still hiding things. A jury isn't going to be very forgiving about any of that, which is why I'm advising you the way I am. Believe me, I'm on your side."

I started to cry. It was like a bright, terrifying light had spread over everything. Doug was right. I had done those things. I had. It wouldn't matter to anyone that I'd done it for someone I loved. Only that I'd done it at all.

He sighed. "Have you got any family that you want me to notify? About Thursday?"

I thought of Grandma, dead. Of Dee, gone too, though I didn't know where. Bird with no idea. Cherry ignorant and not even caring.

I shook my head.

"I'll come see you tomorrow." He nodded with finality. "In the meantime, just think about what I said, and that day, and if there's anything else you might remember that—"

But he stopped there. Because we both knew. We knew there was nothing I could say that would make any of this less bad.

• • • •

When I got to the common room, it was like everything inside me had been squeezed out. And I had absolutely nothing to fill myself back up with. I never would. I could hardly see in front of me. The guards were talking, barely paying attention, and everyone else focused on the TV even if they didn't want to be. The early evening news was all there was, but I didn't care much either way. I was nothing.

Until they showed him on the screen.

I realized I must've made a noise—surprise, I guess, and horror, and delight too, in just seeing his face—when Priscilla came over by me. For a moment my skin buzzed, like his energy was coming through the TV, fueling me. The picture of him was a mug shot, but there was also footage from the police. They were bringing him out of his house and into a police car, his mother in the doorway with her hands over her face.

I tried to focus on what the newscaster was saying: "... still unclear what led to this important breakthrough yesterday, but county police are saying that the arrest of suspect Denarius Pavon is a 'huge milestone' in the case regarding the murder of Deputy Palmer on August twenty-forth. Currently Pavon is being held at the county jail and awaits determination of his bond. A trial date is yet to be set, and investigators tell us they are still compiling evidence in this controversial and very disturbing case. For now, I'm Kelly Douglas, for Channel Two Action News."

I had my hand to my mouth. I only knew it when Priscilla put her own hand on my wrist, urging me to bring it down.

"Killing a cop," she said, calm, "is serious. Everyone's seeing that now."

I knew what she meant. She meant the girls in here but also

the other guys in jail with him now. Some of them proud, sure. Glad the cop was dead. Some of them scared of what he might do. But some of them—maybe most of them—willing to squeal to make things worse.

Suddenly I was filled up again. Filled up to the very edges of everything.

With fear. For Dee.

THE NEXT DAY WAS EVEN HARDER TO GET THROUGH.
Harder to get away from all the thoughts.

Bird, turning away from me.

Dee getting put in that cop car.

My own hand, tossing those guns in the glove box.

Doug telling me I was guilty.

Dee's mouth all over my body, unable to get enough.

Cherry in the doorway, leering, glassy eyed.

Jamelee, so proud of herself, bouncing in that swing.

My own voice, pleading with Dee in the parking lot at his gym.

The blue rest stop sign, moving toward us so fast.

Detective DuPree, writing down everything I said.

That terrible letter, wilted and worn in the plastic bag.

Dee's face—in pleasure. And scowling, too.

Wiping down the inside of Bird's car, so careful.

Kenyetta in the kitchen. And pushing me across the yard.

Dee, smoking a cigarette. Dee, smiling down at me at the fair. Dee, telling me to shut up, lie down, do what he said. Telling me that he loved me.

Dee.

Dee.

Dee.

Dee.

They were calling my name. From under a deep curtain of sleep I heard it, *Nicola Dougherty.* My eyes yanked open. For a minute I thought it was all already over—they were taking me to prison forever. Maybe they'd even kill me. I wondered if I'd already gone to trial and had sleepwalked through the whole thing.

But it wasn't that. It was only the beginning.

In the bunk below, Priscilla shifted but stayed silent. They were calling other names, other girls in the block who had arraignments today too. One of the guards appeared in front of our cell.

"Come on, Nikki. Time to load up."

I didn't know what time it was, but it was earlier than regular wake up. The guard told me to put my hands through the bars so he could cuff me. The metal around my wrists was heavy in an already-familiar way, and I wondered how many more times I was going to be feeling it.

He unlocked the door and slid it open, and I moved out into the hall, where there were four more girls from our block, waiting. Everyone was tired and sleepy, not talking or looking at each other. Serious.

We were led through a series of locked hallways and then out into the yard. It was cooler outside than I expected, and goose bumps leapt along my arms. I hadn't been outside since I got here, and I wasn't sure, feeling the big open air around me—even in this fenced-in space—if I liked it. It was open, but not. Outside, but not. Even the dawning sky looked grim.

We waited. A few other women were led out. It was strange to see people so much older than the rest of us. One of them started talking to a girl from my block. They knew each other. From outside. They were bawdy and laughing, and we could hear everything they said, gossiping about friends who had called in from the outside. It was like they were in the salon instead of jail.

"Ladies, we ain't going nowhere until you all quiet down," the guard said, though more in a reminding way than a mean one.

Another couple of women were brought out, and then a tall, thin guard with a shiny bald head nodded to everyone, and we were told to line up against the wall. I got separated from the others from my block and found myself next to a woman I was surprised to see was pregnant. She saw me glance down at her belly, and she patted it.

"Yeah," she said, smiling a little.

"How long have you been here?" I couldn't help blurting.

"Oh, I didn't get this in here, don't worry." She laughed. "It happened before I knew what a sorry-ass rat bastard her daddy was. Before I hit him in the head with a brick and set fire to his house."

I didn't know what to say to this. Partly because I didn't know if she was lying to seem tough. Was I supposed to ask if he was dead or not, if the house had actually burned to the ground? I didn't know how to chat idly with people about the crimes they'd committed. Didn't know if we were even supposed to discuss anything. Everyone around me had been swapping stories like it was nothing—not even if they were innocent and in here anyway. I still wasn't sure I'd done anything myself. But I definitely didn't know how to be breezy about it. I didn't know what there was to laugh over.

"Wish these bitches would shut up so we could just get on with it," the pregnant woman muttered next to me. "My name's Maya, by the way."

She held out her hand. Nails bitten down, severe.

"I'm Nikki."

"I saw you," she said. "On the TV."

"Oh." It was embarrassing. And a surprise. I wondered if Bird had seen too.

"You really kill that cop?"

"I didn't—"

"Yeah. I get it. Don't worry. I didn't really set fire to Omar's house either."

I nodded, but I noticed she'd left out the part about the brick.

We started moving then, back into the building and down a different hall than the one we came out through. More locked doors, more guard checks and counts, into a giant freight elevator, where we were made to turn around and face the back. Around me everyone was chattering, energized by each other's company. One girl talked loud and proud about how she and her sister tricked for drugs, how bad she was feeling on the detox in here. How she couldn't wait to get this all over with so she could get back to "the life."

"Bullshit loudmouth," Maya whispered beside me as we moved out of the elevator and along another hall, this one leading outside to an underground parking lot where one of those white prison buses was waiting for us, lights blinking on top. "She's just saying all that so people will think she can bring in a score from outside. What she's gonna do is end up getting her ass beat."

"Do you know her?"

"Plenty of fools like her." She looked at me. "This ain't my first time in here, you know."

I nodded, trying not to seem either surprised or too much like I'd expected as much while we took our seats.

Things quieted down on the ride, everyone remembering how tired they were. I watched out the small holes in the metal covering over the window, thinking about what was about to happen. I didn't want to have to say I was guilty, get up there and look like a criminal. But from how Doug explained it, that's what I was. So I might as well get on with it. Begin my new life of everything being over.

We arrived at the courthouse, again in an underground deck, and were led out single file through a hallway and into a smallish auditorium, with rows of wooden benches and a screen set into the wall in front of us. Being in a new place got everyone buzzing again.

"All right, y'all quiet down so we can get started," the tall bald guard said. For a few minutes, though, no one shut up, just kept talking and giggling. Maya grumbled beside me but didn't say anything clear. I wondered if she was uncomfortable, being pregnant and on this wooden bench. I wondered how long we would have to sit here.

After a few more times of being told to quiet down, the room settled, and up on the screen popped a video of an old, bag-eyed judge. He swayed forward and back while he talked, explaining what was going to happen—that we'd be read our charges and asked for our plea. Bail, in some cases, would be amended. The whole thing took much longer than it seemed it needed to, his explaining, and then we had to watch it again, dubbed over in Spanish. It was odd, watching this old white guy with red-rimmed eyes speaking so seriously with Mexican coming out of his mouth. It wasn't enough to be funny, though.

We were told to stand up and that we'd be heading into the courtroom. Absolute silence was demanded. Anybody showing any disrespect would be taken to a holding cell until everyone else had been heard. A curtain of seriousness seemed to fall over everyone's shoulders as we moved down the hall toward the larger room.

It took a long time for the three women ahead of me to get into the courtroom, and when I finally crossed through the door myself, I understood why. Something had gone wrong inside. More guards were against the opposite wall, moving some male prisoners from the hearing before ours through another door. Their faces were tense. I was surprised they were even letting us in. Clearly, it was all a miscommunication that might get someone fired. Or hurt.

As if the tension wasn't already bad enough, across the room someone started yelling. A fight. It felt like everyone behind me squealed and tried to push in to see all at once, but the ones ahead of me had stopped, blocking everyone. One had her hands over her mouth, laughing. Guards started yelling, reaching for pepper spray. Over all the noise a guy was screaming out, "You bitch! You ugly, stupid, worthless bitch! I'll kill you, bitch, I swear I will kill you."

Behind me, two girls got hauled aside by guards. More deputies came in from somewhere, trying to force everyone into order. I wasn't sure if I should stay where I was standing or try to move into a seat. There was so much confusion. You could hear other male prisoners in the outside hall, jeering too. But suddenly, for me, it was like the rest of the room was in silent slow motion. All I could focus on was the guy over there screaming. Two, three guards wrestled him down to the ground. His face was red and the tendons in his neck were tight. His mouth twisted in hate as he yelled over everything, "It was never you! It was never you, you hear me? It never stood for you."

It was so strange, watching him. Like a kind of distorted reality. He looked like a crazy man spitting out nonsense. But at the same time, only I knew that he was making perfect sense.

Because it was Dee there, on the ground. And the bitch he meant was me.

• • • •

I don't remember after that. After I saw them hauling Dee away, his face contorted like that . . . It was like a wall went down in me. On me. In front of me. Something. I heard what was going on, but I couldn't react. Couldn't feel anything at all. The other women in their orange, standing up, hearing their charges read, answering in some way. Different lawyers up there next to them. Even Maya going up to the podium, saying—something—then sitting back down. Doug a row or two behind us, I knew. Watching me. Trying to signal me. But everything inside me was static, white noise. Nothing.

Someone called my name.

Doug stood next to me in his big jacket. Smelling like Old Spice.

The judge read something and asked did I understand.

And I must've somehow said, out loud, *yes*, because more was said. Something about money. And how did I want to plead.

But all I could see was Dee running toward me, between those houses, majestic and brave. Red hair flying. His face cackling with glee, and then collapsing with bliss above me, and finally crumpling, just now, into utter disgust. Over and over I saw him, his face, playing out in front of me in a constant spool.

And the only thing buzzing in my ears: *Bitch, it never stood for you.*

BACK IN JAIL. THE CONFERENCE ROOM. DOUG ACROSS from me, freaking out. Everything in me numb—nothing but hopelessness and shock. Doug asking had I stayed silent on purpose. Did I understand what a not-guilty plea meant, how this made things so much more complicated. I watched his mouth, mostly, his overlapping teeth. Eyebrows that needed to be shaped. Recent shave. His lips moving around in words that came out to me as only, *Bitch*. And, *I hate you*. And, *It never stood for you*.

ANOTHER DAY. I SWAM THROUGH THE FOG IN FRONT OF ME only because I had to. Treading water that had no temperature, only heaviness. Doug came again. Something about more information, talking to more detectives. More evidence. But I couldn't talk to him. He left, frustrated, and the part of me that could pay attention to anything outside of me didn't blame him. But he didn't need to take it personal. I wasn't talking to anyone else around me either. I just followed where the current of the routine was making me go. Wake up. Clean up. Breakfast. Showers. Common room. Lunch. More common time. Outside. Dinner. Reading. Lights-out.

Dark. It was finally dark. But still I could see all those horrible things, hear the words Dee said. I pressed my eyes harder and harder, but it was all still there. And then there was a squeal of metal, and a strong hand went over my mouth. Knees clenched at my rib cage.

"You gotta cut it out." I couldn't see her, but Priscilla's breath was close. "Don't you fucking dare become a ghost in here with me. I'll shove you down the stairs myself. You think you the only one? Sad? Missing? Lonely? Regretful? You're already like an infection. Everybody sees it. That's why no one's talking to you. You need to toughen up and find something to do with yourself. Otherwise you're nothing but a sack of cement in here, sinking. And if you're not careful, we're all going to kick to get away from you. Including me."

She was squeezing my jaw, tight. I could barely breathe. I felt her lean close, closer. Like she was going to bite me. Or kiss me. But she just pressed my face in her hand and lifted my head up, then slammed it down into the pillow. Hard enough to bang the metal underneath.

"You make me sick," she huffed.

Then she was off me and down the ladder, and everything was dark.

DID I SLEEP? NEXT THING, IT WAS LIGHTS ON AGAIN, GUARDS calling. Time for morning cleanup. Without looking at Priscilla, I climbed down from my bunk and took the ammonia bucket, moved around the cell, wiping everything down. I pulled my covers as tight as hers. It took a while, because most of me didn't want to move. And I didn't want to touch or even look at Priscilla.

Something about what she'd said last night must've sunk in, though, because in the showers I realized I could actually feel the water on my skin. Showering was still a strange experience—there were only half walls to the stalls and no doors, and the guards stood watch as we turned back and forth under the spray—but the pounding water felt good against my scalp. The suds flowed down and over my belly, around my ankles. And I could finally feel it.

Of course Dee was still behind my eyes all morning, everywhere. It was impossible to let go of him. But under that— over it?—was Priscilla breathing close to me. The bruise on my ribs that her knees had made. *You're a cement sack, sinking.* I looked over at her, ashamed she thought that. And I knew, innocent as she looked working her crossword puzzle, she had no fear about taking me down before I took her down first.

So I stared at the TV with a few of the other girls, not ready to do anything but at least aware of my surroundings now. Aware of how normal everyone still acted in here, like it wasn't a big thing. Aware that maybe I should start thinking of it that way too.

Somewhere between breakfast and lunch, they called out girls with last names in the first half of the alphabet. Visitors. And they said my name.

Immediately my heart jumped—Bird. Bird had come to see me. The resentment I'd felt toward her immediately melted. All I wanted was to see her face. Even if she hadn't forgiven me fully yet, she was here now. And maybe bringing news about the investigation. Maybe she wanted me to know that turning myself in had gotten them to stop asking her questions. Relief and gratitude washed through me. Bird. I could see her so clearly in my mind it brought tears to my eyes. Bird was here, and everything would be better.

When I got there, I thought they'd brought me to the wrong compartment. Who was this blond hag already crouched over her receiver? Someone else's sister, mother, or friend. But then she looked up. And she was Cherry.

"What are you doing here?" I spoke first.

"I'm not happy to see you either, puss. How you think it feels to a mother, learning from Bo her kid got arrested, thanks only to some goody-goody neighborhood 'This Week's Nabs' sign he saw while buying cigarettes?"

"Someone told me it was on the news."

"Hell if I know whether you were, but that bohunk you used to hang around with sure was. You could hear the cops slapping each other on the back for miles, catching his rotten ass. You know what your bail is?"

I struggled to remember what the judge had said at my hearing. What else Doug told me while he was spazzing.

She didn't care what my answer was, though. "I don't have it, no matter what it is. So, you're just gonna have to sit pretty in here awhile, little miss, till they decide to let you out. You know how long that'll be? Sixty days? Eight months? Whatever it is, you might have to start working on those hand jobs you're so famous for."

She winked at me. My stomach twisted.

"So was it all you? Or just him?"

"They think I . . . I mean I told them that . . ."

She flapped her hand, dismissing me. "It don't matter whichever way, honey. You got a lawyer?"

"Yes, ma'am."

She leaned back. "Ma'am. You're so cute. *Ma'am.* They already got you trained good, huh? Suppose it didn't take too much, after what your old man taught you."

"Gary's not my dad."

She snorted. "May as well be since you take after him so damn much. Here you are, just like him, moping your life in jail, not enough sense not to get caught. You never were enough like me to understand."

I clenched my teeth. "I'm glad I'm not like you."

She laughed. "Oh, big brave girl now, huh? Sassing back? With this thick barrier between you and me?" She rapped her knuckles on the glass. As she leaned forward, I could see straight down the scoop neck of her T-shirt all the way to her still-toned but sun-wrinkled stomach. She sat back, looking at me. Like I was the source of every single thing that had ever displeased her and ever would.

"You got a paycheck you need me to pick up for you at the salon?" she said.

My mind clicked back over the days, feeling a glimmer of hope. I probably did have some money waiting there since we got our hourly pay at the first of the month and again on the sixteenth. It hadn't been ready at my last shift. Alessia probably wondered why I hadn't picked it up.

Hadn't shown up, more like. It hit me then, the other things that might've gone wrong because of me. I'd left Alessia totally in the lurch, for example, with no word at all. She probably called Bird to find out was I okay. And Bird not knowing either. The terrible light shone over me then, showing me more of what I'd done. I hadn't thought people might worry. May have called hospitals, the police. The other girls at the salon would've had to cover my shifts too. Alessia would have to hire someone to take my place. She must think I was a horrible person. Five years working there and I'd just disappeared.

Still, whether she hated me or not, I could really use that money. Even if it was only a couple hundred bucks. Alessia could mail me the check, and I could—my heart sank. You couldn't get money in jail. Someone outside had to deposit it for you into your account. And if I signed over my check to her, Cherry would only keep it. Which is why, I understood, she was asking about it at all.

"Alessia's holding it to cover for the hours I missed," I lied.

"I imagine you owe her quite a bit." Cherry smirked. Then: "You need anything?"

And for a second, she seemed sweet about it. That it worried her, me being here in jail and her not being able to help. If she'd been any other kind of mother, I'd ask her, maybe, to go check on Bird. But I'd never wanted Cherry anywhere near there, and I especially didn't want it now.

This must've showed on my face because she coughed and reached for her bag.

"Well, you keep in touch, darlin'. Tell me what's going on with your case if you can. Maybe I'll come see you. And Emilio says hi."

She didn't say it winky or even mean. She'd probably forgot the whole thing from that night. But she might as well've handed me a glass of pure vomit, gross as it made me feel.

"Good-bye, Cherry," was all I said.

Her face went from a little hurt, back to cold and disapproving. I didn't feel sorry. I didn't feel anything for her. We hung up our receivers at the same time, and our eyes met. She'd said I wasn't like her, but we both had blue eyes, both dishwatery blond hair we tried to make more platinum in our own ways. Both of us disliking each other. Knowing we were linked, regardless.

I went back into the main room without turning around or waving. The only small victory about the whole exchange was picturing what Cherry'd gone through to come and see me.

Because of visits we'd made to Gary in the past, I knew about the pat downs, the inspection—still, it wasn't enough to make any of the things she'd said disappear. It wasn't enough to make seeing her, or any of this, any better.

It was almost lunchtime, and the card-playing girls were snapping at each other to hurry up so they could finish this hand. Priscilla was at her corner table, working her crossword puzzle. I wasn't sure how to talk to her after what she'd done to me in the night, but thinking about Alessia, and everyone outside, gave me an idea. Priscilla was the only one I felt I could ask for any help.

"You got paper?" I said, sliding into the seat across from her.

She looked up at me over the rims of those grandpa glasses of hers.

"I mean," I corrected. "I wondered if you had any paper I could use. Please?"

"You have to get that stuff from the commissary."

I flicked my eyes toward the door that led down the hall to it. We were only allowed to go twice a week, and everything—everything—cost money. I hadn't had a chance to buy anything yet, because it'd taken a while for them to transfer the few bucks I'd come in with, but I knew that unless I got a job, I wasn't going to have enough for more than about one visit in there.

"Course, they have class," she said. "Sometimes you can get materials in there."

"I'm not signed up for anything. I don't know how. I don't even know when it is."

She was so still. Unreadable as a bar of soap.

"Tuesdays."

"What day is today?"

Her eyes rolled. "Today's Sunday, dumbass. You didn't hear them announcing service if you wanted to go? Jesus. You haven't even been here a week. But that's long enough to know a hell of a lot more than you do."

"I'm sorry. I really am. But I'm trying to be . . . smarter."

"You need to. Quick."

She sounded the way she had last night.

"That's what I'm trying. Why I'm asking you for some paper. You said I should find something to do. And I have something. I just—don't have everything I need for it."

The guards called for lunch then. Priscilla stood up, folded her newspaper in half and clipped her pen to it, neat.

"You need to think how to pay me."

Picking at a few grisly chicken nuggets and what they were calling vegetable soup, I considered what I could possibly offer Priscilla. I didn't know what she needed—I didn't even know how long she'd been in here, though it seemed like a while. She was right: it was stupid how much I didn't know, how out of touch I had been with the reality of my own life. There was so much she had and knew, and so much I didn't. Money. Smarts. A routine.

Friends.

After lunch there was an opportunity to go outside for exercise, if you wanted, but I still didn't like the idea of it. When they came back, Priscilla sat next to where I was reading that same beat-up paperback, feeling sorry for myself in sixteen ways. She slid a half piece of notebook paper over to me. With a pen.

I didn't ask her where they came from. I didn't ask her what I was going to have to do. I just nodded, said, "Thank you," and hoped the rest would come.

Dear Jamelee . . .

I'd thought of writing Alessia first, to apologize and explain, tell her to keep my money, but staring at the paper, all I could picture was Jamelee's tight mossy curls. Her delighted-with-herself giggle. Her fat little hands, petting Bird, tired.

> *You may have noticed I haven't been around,*
> *and your momma may have told you about this*
> *already, but the reason is that I'm in jail.*

I still wasn't sure if Bird already knew, or if this letter would be her way of finding out.

> *It isn't as bad as I was afraid of, but it isn't exactly*
> *nice either. I want you to do all you can to make*

*sure you never end up here. I know your momma
will work toward that too.*

I paused again, smiling a little, thinking of Bird reading that and laughing in her low, hesitant way. I couldn't pause for too long, though. Too long and I would stop.

*I want you to know that I miss you and that I'm
sorry for leaving you. Sometimes there are things
you just have to do, though. Even if you can't
explain them right, to yourself or anyone else,
they're what you have to do. So that you can, in
some way, hold on to what you love. Everyone
else may think it's wrong, but they don't always
understand you. And just because you're not
understood doesn't mean you're wrong. Unless
maybe you one day end up thinking it's wrong
yourself too.*

I wanted to start over, but I kept going.

*It's hard to know all the time what's good and
what's bad. Everyone says you have to decide for
yourself, but what do you do if yourself doesn't
know? If yourself only feels that people will turn
against you unless you give them what they want,
and even then somewhere inside you you know*

they will still turn on you, still hurt you and leave
you? What I'm saying is, sometimes, things get
mixed up. And you don't know where to turn. You
don't even have your own self to rely on because
you're just a mixed-up bag of worthlessness. To you
or anyone. And I want you to know, Jamelee, that
if you ever need to, even though I'm not there right
now—you can turn to me.

I read the whole thing over. I'd started out writing pretty big, but by the end it was all scrunched up together along the bottom inch. It wasn't the kind of thing to write to a baby at all. And it wasn't exactly what I wanted to say to Bird either. But, writing it, I felt . . . if not better, at least . . . something. Even simply letting my eyes blur, staring at the inky lines on the page—something about the whole thing felt good.

I didn't try to change it around too much. I wasn't sure if I was going to send it at all, and I didn't have more paper. For today, I was done. I slid the pen back over to Priscilla and folded the piece of paper into thin sections. I tucked the folded-up letter into the saggy elastic of my sports bra. I would read it again later.

THE NEXT MORNING, DURING CLEANUP, IT SUDDENLY CAME over me what I could do to pay back Priscilla. Her, and maybe anyone else I needed a favor from. It was foolish I hadn't thought of it before. All it took was Priscilla bending to make her bed and me seeing that thick ponytail of hers held back with elastic she plucked out of her jail-issue underwear.

"I can give you braids, if you want."

She didn't say anything, just kept at her sheets: tucking everything just so. Then she stood up. "What, like Laura Ingalls Wilder?"

I didn't know who she was talking about. But it didn't sound good.

"Like whoever you want. It's what I do—did—out there. Before."

She stared at me. Archie came to collect our cleaning things. I handed him the bucket and rags and followed Priscilla out to the dining hall for breakfast. I didn't know what was going to happen next.

PRISCILLA DIDN'T COME OVER TO GET HER HAIR FIXED right away. Mainly because first there was commissary: everyone getting forms passed out to fill out with what we wanted. It was the first time I'd seen the list, and I was curious. Everyone was talking about what they were going to get, what they needed, one girl with acne scars and bad teeth yakking how she was about to be on the rag and the jail-issue tampons never soaked up her flow good enough.

Just scanning my eye down the list, I could practically smell Dorito cheese, could see the sugar clinging to the plastic wrap of those Little Debbies and frosted Danish. All the things I used to buy and pick up without thinking. Now it was like they were treasure. But I forced myself to focus on other things. My own non-jail-issued toothbrush, for example, and more toothpaste. Priscilla had been sharing hers without saying anything about it, but it was plain her charity toward me was wearing thin. I checked both those off and also a box of better tampons, though I didn't know for sure when mine was supposed to come. That was one of the most expensive things on the list. So much else was food. Junk food, but food that was way better than what they gave us. My mouth had felt full of sand for about the last week, but suddenly it was watering, thinking of Nutter Butters and Easy Macaroni and Cheese.

Still, I barely had any money. Maybe fifteen dollars, total. Almost half of it was used up just with these three things, and I didn't know when I was going to get more.

Maybe I would get a job. Some of the girls had them—they got called out at different times in the mornings and the afternoons, evenings when other girls went to AA and NA meetings—but I hadn't figured out how any of those things worked yet. It seemed if you wanted something in here, you had to go after it yourself. And I hadn't been able to do much of anything so far.

Luckily, the other things I did want were on the list and not as expensive as I expected. A letter pad for only $2.50 and ballpoint pens for eighty-five cents apiece. I put myself down for two. One to give to Priscilla, just for.

There were other things I would need. Envelopes, for one. But I thought I'd see if I could trade for them first. Handing in my form, trying to do some more mental math just to figure out what money I had left, the only other thing I could think about was what I would say to Jamelee next. It was like the thoughts were forming in my mind before I even started writing. I could see the shapes of what I wanted to say without knowing the exact words. There was a feeling in me that wasn't quite what you call excited, but it was definitely . . . interesting. And that was a far better feeling than any I'd had in here yet.

IT WAS IN THE LATE AFTERNOON DURING *JUDGE JUDY*—THE girls watching talking so much to each other and the TV, it was a wonder they could hear the show at all—that Priscilla came over with two of her friends.

"This is Bindi." She motioned to the tiny, dusk-skinned girl who I'd seen playing cards. I remembered she had a loud, sharp laugh but was otherwise quiet. "And this is Cam." Cam was Bindi's opposite: tall—mannish tall—with a surfer girl face, freckled peachy skin, and a blond bob. She'd sat on Priscilla's other side at meals for days now, but I had yet to really talk to her, to any of them.

"So, my hair?" Priscilla raised doubtful eyebrows at me. She had a hairbrush.

I smiled. An actual one. "Come here and sit down." I took out a chair and pulled it alongside the table. "Do you care what I do?"

"Just don't make me any uglier than I already am."

I ignored her—all three of them were eight times prettier than me—and spent some time just raking my fingers lightly over her hair, getting the feel of what she had. When I finally picked up the brush, it was hard getting through the tangles. After a few minutes of watching me, though, Bindi jumped up and asked for permission to go get something. She came back with a small jar of pomade and a cheap but better-than-nothing comb. I put a bit of the pomade on the comb and used it to slowly smooth out Priscilla's thick locks. It felt like it took forever, but when I was done combing everything out, I wanted to leave it just the way it was—wavy-smooth and slightly shiny—but that wasn't what I'd promised. Besides, Cam and Bindi were sitting backward in chairs, watching me as I worked. It was like doing hair in front of little girls, the way they were so transfixed.

The idea of goddess braids came first, but since I'd never worked with Priscilla's hair before, something simpler seemed better. I separated out some strands at the top of her head and started plaiting. Pretty soon, I fell into the rhythm of what I was doing, and I hardly noticed anything or anyone else.

"You look good," I told Priscilla when I'd finished. It was

like coming out of a daze, stepping back and taking in my work.

I hadn't done the tightest or smoothest braid ever. At the salon I'd been mostly doing straightenings or weaves, so I was a little rusty at this kind of do, but it was nice. A French braid started at the top left of Priscilla's head and then crossed over to the right, then moved down and around left again, and then back across the bottom of her head, in an S shape. I hadn't done something like that since middle school, probably. I was impressed my fingers had remembered.

Cam clapped and Bindi smiled.

"You can't do that with mine, can you?" Bindi said, looking at the thin end of her long, straight ponytail.

I frowned. "I wish I had some pins. And some hair spray."

"We can get you some," Cam said hopefully, but then her eyebrows came together. "Or some rollers at least. I forget what we can have." She looked at Priscilla.

"No hair spray, that's for sure."

"It's all right," I said. "What I really need are some stamps."

THE NEXT DAY I GAVE CAM CORNROWS. WE USED THREADS she pulled out from the unraveling hem of her T-shirt to tie off the ends. It took forever, but while I was working, about four or five other girls came to sit around and watch, talk. I asked Cam why she was in here—I didn't know most of the girls' stories at all—and she laughed and told how she'd tried to hold up a convenience store with her boyfriend when they were both high on meth. The cashier had gone for something under the counter—she said she had no idea what, but the motion scared her—and she'd shot him in the shoulder. Her boyfriend was so freaked he just dropped everything and ran. So Cam ran out with him. The police found them only a few hours later, back at home smoking more to calm down. The way she told it, it was like she was telling a story about somebody else—someone she couldn't believe could ever be that dumb. Part of me wanted to jump in and say it wasn't her fault. That it had just been the drugs. But I didn't have even that to blame in my own situation, and I could relate anyway. So I kept quiet.

Besides that, I had to concentrate. It was harder doing cornrows on white girl hair than I remembered, and Cam couldn't keep still. But when I was done, she ran to the bathroom to look and came out beaming. So I guess I did okay.

Bindi was next up. And she was less talkative about her crime than Cam.

"My roommate and I got in a fight, and she . . . cut herself. She was in the hospital. She told everyone it was me. And since no one else was there, I—"

Cam reached over and squeezed Bindi's hand, told her it was okay. I finished up braiding and could already see, because her hair was just so thin and slippery, that it was all going to fall out before too long, but I hoped it would stay nice as long as it could.

Two other girls asked me could I do theirs after lunch, and even one of the woman guards seemed curious. So, after everyone took their time outside in the yard, I did hair all afternoon. I laughed, heard stories, and thought about trying to do this for some kind of job if I was going to be here long enough. I hadn't seen Doug since just after the hearing, and most of what he'd told me was a blur, but from what the other girls were saying about their own time here, I knew it could be a long wait.

For once, the day went by pretty fast. After dinner, I tried to write to Jamelee while Priscilla and a bunch of others went to the nightly AA meeting. After several tries though, I hadn't gotten anywhere. Writing about the day, and my new friends, made life in here seem almost normal. Normal like I used to have with Bird, helping her in her kitchen, cutting up with Kenyetta or whoever. Remembering how my real life used to be—picturing what she'd have to say about these women I was wanting to think of as my friends—made me miss Bird in a shadowy place just under the edges of my ribs. And missing Bird made me miss Dee.

To forget both of them, I watched TV with everyone instead. Before lights-out—as we were cleaning things up in the common room and getting ready to head off to brush our teeth—Bindi slipped past, handed me two envelopes and a book of stamps.

IN THE MORNING, I LOOKED AT THE THREE LETTERS I'D written to Jamelee. I wasn't sure if Bird, seeing where they were from, would even open them. I thought for a long time about not sending them at all. I could keep them, maybe, and give them to Jamelee when I was out. When she was older. But that didn't feel right either. So I folded them up quick and stuck them in the envelope, wrote Bird's address, fast. Nervous as it made me, uncertain as I was about what they said or why I'd even written them, I knew they had to go out in the world.

THAT AFTERNOON A NEW PRISONER GOT TRANSFERRED into our block. Right away, the other girls started giggling and fussing over her. Priscilla muttered that it was probably because she'd snuck in pills, which made me feel extra strange about paying her any attention, but when Bindi led her over to me, I told her to sit down. Asked her what she wanted me to do to her hair.

I wasn't too long into it when a guard called for me. Because Doug was here.

The guard took me to the same conference room where I'd met him before. Right away he stood up. I didn't know how to feel, seeing him. Was he mad at me? Did he want to stop being my lawyer? I looked at him for clues. His face was small, pale.

Suit still too big for him. The guard shut the door behind her, stood outside, and watched us through the glass window.

"Hello, Nikki."

"Doug."

He started talking, and pretty quick I realized this time I was actually following what he was saying. He seemed to notice and relaxed more. After what had happened at my arraignment, he explained, things became complicated. Refusing to speak, even after being prompted by both Doug and the judge (which I didn't really remember), was the same as a not-guilty plea. Which meant I was going to have to go through a trial.

"And, in this case, unless there's proof that you were truly coerced by Mr. Pavon at the time or out of your mind on drugs, though even then nothing's guaranteed—"

He stopped, looking at me. Hoping I would say it had been drugs. That maybe I didn't even remember that day, really. Didn't remember ever talking to the detectives. He was hoping I'd tell him I'd done it because—but I didn't know what. The only drug I'd been on was love. The only thing that made me insane was my desire to please Dee. And I knew, even if it was true, that wasn't going to hold up in any kind of court.

Doug saw the expression on my face and went on. "I'm just not sure there's a lot for us to do, Nikki, to be honest. I mean, I'll defend you, of course, to the best of my abilities. I've already gotten some background information on Mr. Pavon, and I can certainly demonstrate that you were under an incredibly bad influence. Gang background. Prior suspect in another murder. Robbery. But with these lies of yours, Nikki, and the confession, with a jury . . ."

His eyes met mine.

But it was hard to think past the other things he'd said about Dee: "prior murder," "gang background," and "robbery." It was bringing Dee too close to me again, and I didn't want to see any of it. I couldn't cling to the need of him—not if I wanted to survive—but this new bright reality was too much. I still wanted at least a tiny scrap of the old him left for me to hold on to, to love.

"That's why I've arranged a meeting," Doug said, pulling out papers from his briefcase.

"A meeting?"

"With the lawyers for the state. They're moving as fast as they can. And they want to talk to you."

I didn't know what he was getting at. He saw my confusion and nodded.

"These aren't the lawyers who will eventually be prosecuting you, Nikki. They're prosecuting Mr. Pavon. What you told the police was helpful in arresting him, but they feel you might have more information. They'd like to know what it is because they think your story might truly convince a jury of his guilt. Put him behind bars forever. Talking to them could . . ." He cleared his throat, wiped his hands on the table in front of him. "It could dramatically affect your own sentencing, Nikki, if you gave them a full, truthful testimony. As of now, you're still going to be tried for your part in this murder, no matter what you tell them. You've got to remember that. What you've told the police so far doesn't make anything look good for you in that case. But you could make it look a lot worse for him. And, in the long run, that might help you."

I was shocked. How did they know there was more to say? And how could I tell them everything anyway? The idea of discussing that Saturday again—with anyone—brought the sound of gunshots back. Dee's crazy laugh. His pride and gratitude. His hands all over me. I'd managed not think about him much, not after a while. And now he was here. Here, and filling up the room. Needing my loyalty more than ever.

"Will you talk with them? Hear what they have to say? As your lawyer"—Doug smiled in a sad way—"I would definitely advise it."

I didn't want to. Wasn't going to. Not just for Dee's sake, but because things had been so nice lately. Not nice, exactly, but . . . easier. Dee's fury felt put away for a while. All of it did. I didn't want it—or anything about him—to come any closer. Not in here. Not when I was trying to be normal. When I'd just started thinking about Bird and how to get her to forgive me.

But Doug's face said I didn't have much choice in the matter. So after a minute of thinking—not thinking—I told him I guessed I would.

"Okay, good," he said. "Because they're here."

RIGHT AWAY I DIDN'T LIKE HER. THE STATE PROSECUTOR against Dee. She was tall. Too tall. Shoulders like a football player, stuffed into that burgundy suit. Long-fingered hands, with no polish on the nails. Skin the color of parchment paper and hair in a million tiny dreads, pulled back and tied at the nape of her neck. Dark freckles clustered in two crescents under her eyes, like war paint.

Her giant hand dwarfed mine. She had a grip like a construction worker.

"Miss Dougherty, I'm Marjorie Hampton. Have a seat, will you?"

I took the chair she indicated, across from everyone: her, Doug, and a younger woman, also in a suit. Though they hadn't bothered me while I was talking to Doug before, I suddenly hated the fluorescent lights in here, the standard-issue office table. Everything felt darker now, full of more judgment.

The younger woman reached across the table to shake my hand, introducing herself as Bianca Pousner. When I glanced at her face, she gave me a small smile, told me to sit down. Nicely. More like asked. I thought she was my age, maybe, but then of course she couldn't be because she was a lawyer and not a dropout.

"Are you comfortable?" she asked.

The main prosecutor cut over her: "You can call me whatever you're comfortable with. This is Bianca, if you like."

She was trying to smile like this was a favor she was doing.

"What would you like for us to call you?" Bianca said.

"Nikki." My voice was a small noise.

"All right, Nikki," Marjorie said. Though I felt better thinking of her as Hampton. "You do understand the charges against you?"

"Yes, ma'am."

I watched her long, naked fingers spread out the papers in front of her.

"Good. And I hope you've been adjusting all right?"

"I guess so, ma'am."

"Splendid." But she didn't sound so. "Well, as Mr. Jacobsen

may have explained, we are part of the team involved in prosecuting Denarius Pavon in the alleged murder of Deputy Palmer. Do you understand that?"

"Yes, ma'am."

Even the sound of Dee's name brought flashes in me.

"And, since you yourself were an alleged participant, we have some questions for you about what happened on August twenty-fourth, as well as events on the day leading up to it. And after."

I could feel her eyes on me. Feel them even though I couldn't see her through the curtain of other things I was seeing. Him. Me. The yellow house.

"It's important that I let you know that cooperation in this case against Mr. Pavon could possibly have an effect on your own sentencing if the judge decides to be lenient with you. But I want to be clear that I am not here to offer you any kind of deal."

Then I could look at her. Briefly.

"That will remain solely up to the judge who hears your case. Right now, we're here to see if you're willing to answer some questions. Because there are some gaps in the information we have that I think you could be of help with."

When I looked at Doug, he was nodding for the prosecutor to go on.

She held up a paper filled with cop's handwriting. What I'd told them the day they arrested me.

"I understand that this is your statement to the police about the events on August twenty-fourth. Is that correct?"

I couldn't remember anymore what it said on that paper. But her tone of voice, and Doug's hopeful posture gave me no choice. "Yes, ma'am."

"And you know, as well as I do, that this statement clearly implicates you in the murder of Deputy Palmer and is also full of gaps?"

Her face seemed carved of concrete. Hard. Disapproving. Full of distrust. She hated me. She hated what I had done, and she wasn't hiding it.

"That's my statement," I managed to say.

She cleared her throat and shifted in her chair.

Then Bianca took over, leaning toward me in a friendly way. "The thing is, Nikki, we've reviewed all the evidence that's come in so far. But if there's anything you think is missing . . . anything you need to add or want us to know, now's the time. To be honest, we need to know as much as possible."

I stared down at my hands. Without thinking, I had been picking at a chipped edge of my old nail polish. I wasn't really aware of doing it even as I watched myself.

"We need to know—what we're asking you—is if there's more detail you can remember."

I chipped more and more away from my nail. Bird had done

them for me before any of this happened. Hampton shifted in her chair and let out a long breath. Almost like she was about to say something.

"For example," Bianca pressed, "you say that on the morning of the twenty-fourth, you and the accused, Denarius Pavon, were staying at your friend's house. Your friend, let's see . . ."

"Bird didn't have anything to do with any of this," I blurted. "You have to believe me that she didn't know anything. No one needs to question her any more."

I could feel Bianca watching me. But I didn't want to see her face. I was remembering Dee. And me. The sweaty smell of the futon. His telephone on the floor, chiming, *Dooooom. Dooooooom. Doooom.* Bird with her mouth full of pins, concentrating on Kenyetta's dress. Knowing nothing. Trusting me.

"Nikki—" Hampton's voice showed she was already tired of me. "What Bianca is trying to say is that we know you've lied already to the police, on more than one occasion, and we know there are reasons why you might continue to lie to us now. Or, at least, withhold information."

I couldn't say anything to that. I didn't know if I had to, really. I'd told them basically what had happened. I was already here in jail. From what Doug was telling me, I was going to get punished no matter what I did or said anyway. They had Dee too. They had my whole life. I was here for a murder I still didn't really think I'd committed. And now they wanted me to tell them more? To make sure the man I'd loved—even if he didn't care anymore—would rot in prison forever? Did they really think that little of me?

Bianca leaned over and whispered something then to Hampton, who flicked her eyes at me and nodded.

"Nikki, are you aware"—Hampton straightened up—"that Mr. Pavon had a two-year relationship with the victim's daughter, Nicole Palmer? And that as recently as the day he was arrested, he was calling her?"

I flushed. Two years? The tattooed *N* swam before my eyes.

"That's impossible. We started dating in October. And he didn't—"

But it was like she didn't hear me or care what I had to say. "Did you also know that on May twelfth of this year, a restraining order was filed against Mr. Pavon? By Deputy Palmer? To keep him from seeing Nicole?"

May. My breathing stopped. Dizzy swirls crossed my vision. Dee had texted me right around Memorial Day weekend. Appearing from nowhere, after we'd been broken up for months. Bird and I had taken Jamelee out to Stone Mountain and I'd left my phone at home. When we got back, I found that message. Saying he'd been missing me. Wanting to know how I was and could I go see a movie or something. The end of May.

"Detectives confiscated the Palmer family computer, and they found e-mails between Mr. Pavon and Miss Palmer as recent as the month before the murder. Even though we haven't gone through everything yet, I can tell you the basic nature of them is certainly . . . romantic."

Her slimy tone slipped between the cracks of me. The month before the murder. July. Dee'd taken me to watch fireworks at Lenox Mall. He'd poured wine coolers into Gatorade bottles before we left Bird's to make sure we wouldn't get caught drinking in the parking lot. We'd made out on a blanket, not caring about families sitting five feet from us. He'd driven me back—late—and I'd wanted him to stay over. But he was tired, he said. Had to work out in the morning. And then I didn't hear from him for a week.

"I'll also tell you," Hampton went on, shifting gears but keeping her voice pointed, "that there are witnesses. More than one of them reported seeing two people in the vehicle at the scene of the crime. A man and a woman. Neighbors also described a purple Mustang, with a distinctive symbol on the back. The one we now know belongs to your friend—"

"Bird." Her name was lead in my mouth.

But it was like she didn't hear me. "There were also gun casings at the scene of the crime. Over a dozen of them. From two guns: one nine millimeter and another from a forty-five.

Police found a nine millimeter registered under Mr. Pavon's name when they searched his house. The other weapon has yet to be found."

I could see the gun like it was in my hand this minute. Wiping it off with the edge of my shirt. I knew they were trying to scare me, making me think they could imply that I was the one who actually fired it. And for a minute or two, I felt like I had.

But Hampton kept going. "Ms. Dougherty, we know by his phone records that Mr. Pavon and Nicole Palmer had lengthy phone calls on August ninth, twelfth, and fourteenth. That he called her on the day he was arrested. We know, from those same phone records and your own admission, that you and Mr. Pavon were also actively involved at the time. You called him often. You told the police he stayed at Ms. Brown's home with you. It's clear that you also had a romantic relationship."

I didn't want any more of this. Not her questions, not the memories, and, most of all, not the falling, sinking feeling that was starting to swallow me down. My hands were shaking. All of me was shaking. Because I was starting to understand the real reason why he'd done this. Done it because he thought it meant he would be with her. Used me to help just because he knew I'd do anything he said. And no amount of anything was going to make it an easier truth to swallow.

I covered up my face.

The prosecutor's voice was kinder this time: "I understand that this is probably upsetting to you, Nikki, but it would help me to at least know whether you had any knowledge of Mr. Pavon's relationship with Ms. Palmer and if there was anything he said or did—either before that day or during it—that might help us?"

She don't have nothing to do with us.

I didn't say it out loud, but it was all I could think. She didn't have nothing to do with us, but she had everything.

Restraining order. E-mails as recent as July. Phoning her up until the day he got arrested. And it was her *Daddy* who was dead. Killed by Dee to get him out of the way so that the two of them could be together. *You'll be my wife.*

I started to cry. I couldn't help it.

I cried so hard I couldn't talk.

THEY HAD TO END THE MEETING. I WAS CRYING SO MUCH I made myself throw up, and everyone cleared out of the office. Outside, in the hall, Hampton and Bianca told me they knew this was difficult, but their faces didn't seem that way. They shook hands with Doug and said they'd make another appointment if I was willing to talk to them more. After they left, Doug tried to soothe me a little, saying he knew that it was hard, but that this would be really important for a lot of reasons. His hand patted between my shoulder blades a few times. I'd stopped crying, but I'd stopped talking, too. I was too exhausted. I needed everything to disappear. Especially myself.

"I'll give you time to think about it," he told me. "Just call me when you've considered what you want to do. You can take as long as you need."

I nodded, I guess. Said something. Next thing, a guard was there unlocking things, taking me back to the common room. I felt like I could hardly lift my feet, following her. And I didn't want to see anyone.

"Keep your chin up," she said as we went through the door.

But I felt too mean and dead inside for it to sink in she was being nice.

NO ONE WAS IN THE COMMON ROOM. THE GUARD TOOK ME straight to my cell, where Priscilla was already. Pissed-offness poured out of her like steam.

"What happened?" we both wanted to know of each other at the same time. Her, seeing my blotchy, destroyed face, me, wondering why everyone was locked up in their cells in the middle of the day.

"Exactly what I told you," she started right in. "That new girl Dew'ann. Contraband from wherever she came from. Snuck in, whatever. Doesn't matter where she got it. Didn't take them but an hour or two to pin it down. Loudmouths." She shook her head. "And now the rest of us have to stay here, God knows how long. Cell search too."

For no reason, I felt relieved I'd mailed off those letters to Jamelee. From my stepfather, I knew every piece of anything that went in and out of here was read by someone, but it felt better knowing they were reading it as part of an official process instead of finding them among my private things. Treating them like some sort of *discovery*.

That was about as good as I could feel, though.

Priscilla was hunched over on the edge of her bunk. "What they do to you?"

Flashes went before my eyes. Dee pushing up off me, walking into the kitchen. The detectives coming to the salon. Those cops turning things over in Bird's car. That plastic sample bag. Hampton's unforgiving hands, the words that wouldn't stop coming out of her: Dee and that girl Nicole together for two years. The whole time he was with me, lying. Leaving me and going to her. Maybe every single day.

"I don't want to talk about it."

She grunted. "Talking's all there's gonna be for a while."

"Yeah, but I ain't gonna."

I pulled myself up the two railings to my top bunk, lay down. I crossed my hands over my eyes that wouldn't stop seeing.

Dear Jamelee—

    It's been lockdown for hours, and there isn't much else to do, so I might as well warn you: there are things in people that are dark and mean. I don't necessarily want you to curl yourself up away from them—from people—but it's my job to tell you this now. The ones you love will turn their backs on you. They will plot against you even as you love and care for them, give them everything inside you. You will do the most hateful things for them, and you won't even know those things are wrong because you believe in that person so much. In their love for you.

    But let me be a lesson to you. People are snakes inside. Most of them, anyway. Your momma ain't one. But mine is. And others, too. They are snakes who will not think twice about squeezing everything they can out of you, then swallowing you whole. They will take and take and take from you for their own gain. They will smile as you writhe in pain. And they will get away with it if you let them.

HOURS IN THE CELL. LYING THERE. WAITING. WRITING A little bit and then not being able to write. Priscilla working at her crossword puzzle but then getting mad, breaking the tip of her pencil, cussing. We only had each other to talk to, but I still didn't want to talk. After I figured out there wasn't anything more I could say to Jamelee, I just lay there in the bunk, staring at the ceiling. There was so much to think of. Unwanted things, and not just about this life in jail. Things I'd forgot before. They kept coming over me, spilling one on top of the other. Things like the very beginning, when I very first met Dee in that Ferris wheel line at the county fair—how he smiled so sly, got me to give him my number even though I was sure a boy who looked like him asking a girl who looked like me for my number was some kind of prank. My surprise when he called, a day later. Talking slick like I was something expensive he wanted to make sure and win. And then movies. Dinners. A hand on my thigh that wasn't about an exchange. Just wanting. Wanting me and only me. Only that. For a while. Until December, when all the questions everyone else was asking me started coming out of my mouth: When were we gonna get married? What was his intention? What did he think about our future? And then him gone. My phone empty and dead for months. No more questions from me because all there was on the other end was his silence. His refusal.

Bird filling the gap. Helping me every day and letting me help her. Dealing with breakfast and dinner and the baby, plus getting to work. Making things happen. Showing me sometimes you just had to fake it because that was all there was to do. Reminding me there were more immediate problems like the phone bill and the mortgage and getting the baby to sleep and all the other business that just took over anything else, no matter how badly you wanted to let other things swallow you. No matter how far you wanted to sink.

Then May. May and Dee coming around again. Waking me from some kind of coma. Every inch of me electric, in a way I didn't fully understand had got switched off when he left the first time. All from the sound of his voice. A stream, after that, of seeing him. Sex all the time. Everywhere. Like he couldn't get enough. Except for when he disappeared for no reason. And me this time keeping my mouth shut, not asking questions. Because questions only end up in your ass getting left.

Fighting with Bird. Or, more, living with her silence. She hated him, I knew. Even more so when he came back and I didn't kick him to the curb. But she never really took it out on me. She went to work, paid the bills. Insisted I do it too, even after weekends that he spent over and I felt wrung out in more ways than one.

He'd gotten that tattoo while we were broke up. The *N* with the angels. He pulled his shirt over his head the first time we were going to make love again, and I saw it and I didn't say anything. I just knew, without talking, that it was for me. I saw it, and everything swirled gorgeous. *It means something,* I told myself. *We aren't wrong to be in love.* I felt like, looking at that tattoo, that every mistake I'd ever made before or since could be wiped away with those few sweeps of ink. He loved me. It was in his skin. Permanent.

But now, lying on my bunk in our cell, I knew it was for her. Never for me, like he said. He got it for her after we split up, and then he lay in my bed and let me think that it was for me.

I knew I shouldn't, but I pictured them dating. Finding each other online, maybe. Swapping photos and texts. Planning a place to meet. Dinners. Movies. Afternoons at the mall. Her father—a policeman who focused on gangs—being suspicious right away. Becoming more sure something was wrong just by the sound of her voice whenever she talked about Dee. Probably the two of them had to start sneaking. Which made it even more romantic. *Baby. I love you. I want you so bad.* She would've been just as in love with him as I ever was. Weak with him. Overpowered. Falling into the backseat of anywhere, just like I did.

I guess eventually they needed to appease her father, cool things off. This must've been when he found me the first time. Early fall. But after those few months he couldn't take it, being away from her. And he just dumped me on the side of the road like trash. Ran back to her. More intense. Got that tattoo. Together for another few breathless months before her father found out and told her she couldn't see him anymore. Told Dee the same thing. I pictured a fight between them, maybe even with fists. A restraining order. Keeping them apart. And then . . . me. Dee coming around to find me again. Me with no hesitation, despite what Bird had taught me. He knew before he even called that I would do whatever he said, whatever he wanted. I could hear him telling her, Nicole, the same thing. Because the whole time, he was seeing her still. Sneaking behind me. Texting to her in the dark. Maybe even while I was there next to him in bed, asleep. Soothing her as she said how hard it was, her daddy's hatred for him. Asking him to make it better. Giving him an idea. A chance to get her daddy out of the way.

And me being there—the one to help him.

Me here in jail now.

I wiped my tears with the back of my arm. It was morning and they still weren't letting us out. I was sad and tired from all the thinking and crying and hardly any sleep, but also I was angry. I didn't even know what Nicole looked like, but I could see her in my mind. Picture her feeling some sense of victory. That she had no daddy anymore, that no one was looking out for her, meant she was really free now. She could do whatever she wanted.

I stewed. This girl, Nicole, had to've known about it, I thought. The killing. It had to be her idea. How else would Dee have known exactly when the deputy was coming home that day if she hadn't told him? Why else would he have picked that weekend, when she just happened to be out of town? It was her. It was her who came up with the whole thing. I knew it so clearly and so hard I felt certain that everyone else in the whole jail must know it too. Her. Her. It was like a laser beam piercing the middle of my brain, a vision of her calculating the entire thing. Begging him. Cajoling him. Whispering it to him while they lay together. It was her and it was her and it was her. And I knew it.

But they weren't asking me about her. They were asking

me about Dee. It was Dee they wanted to know about. What, exactly, he had done that day.

And I'd already told them. Some of it. But I hadn't told them everything. I hadn't told them about the wigs, how he asked me for them weeks beforehand—clearly plotting. I hadn't told them how he'd changed clothes to throw people off. I hadn't confirmed the exact kinds of guns. I hadn't mentioned the crazy laugh on his face when it was all over, how excited he was. Or how he'd taken me to that rest stop. How, just after he'd killed a man, we'd had sex right there in the back of Bird's car.

I could tell them a lot of things. And they wanted to know. Needed me to tell them so they could lock him up forever for what he did. Telling them might help me too. Make me look better to the judge. But if I told them all of it—if I told them every single thing—it would make me more than the criminal I already was. It would make me a snitch.

The thing was, though, I had done these things with him. I'd helped him with the entire plot, even if I hadn't known it.

And until now, I hadn't even felt that bad about it.

THAT NIGHT—AFTER A WHOLE DAY IN LOCKDOWN—I WAS drifting between sleep and not-sleep, and I had a memory of Dee so strong and sharp it strangled my heart. Him reaching for me. His fingers digging into the soft of my upper arm, the flesh of my waist. Squeezing. Squeezing it out of me—the wanting. Moving quietly, only the sound of cloth on cloth or skin. The sheets. My shorts down my leg. His T-shirt over his head. His hand, pressing. Kneading. Needing. His body so hard—all of him, hard—and mine so soft. Remembering, I could almost still feel where he was ungiving and I was not. His chest over mine. His pelvis against the pads of me. In. Out. Tugging. Everything about him pushing or pulling or fighting. Even his mouth a hard muscle. But warm. And the warm was all I wanted. Because it was a warmth that wasn't about money, or drugs, or any of Cherry's promises—it was just about me and him. I wanted to give him what was warm in me, to offer him a place of fire when everything else in him could be so cold. His eyes. The clenching in him as he turned his face away from mine, breathed "ungh." Always close enough to my ear to distort the sound, so I could make it "baby" or "angel." Him pushing my knees up toward my shoulders, my whole body open, nowhere to hide, and me just wanting him to take it all for himself. To give him comfort. And to fill me up so that I wouldn't have any more room for stupid, ugly, disappointing me. My own body far away from me, only close to him. Him. He'd pull my hair—fingers raking my skull. Everything squeezing. And then, a deep press, and sigh, and rest. I was something of worth then. I had given to him, and he had taken, and we were both complete.

Until he moved off me, away. My skin—where his was no longer touching it—immediately feeling cold. His shirt on over his head again. Standing up, going to the bathroom, lighting a cigarette. I'd still be there on the bed, my everything open, and he'd just take it and walk away.

I saw it all the way it really was then. Me giving and giving, and him not really caring what I was giving him. Because it was never about love for him. And, if I was honest, for me either. Because I was taking too—always taking as much as I could, stuffing myself with him. Cramming him into every space.

But now here I was alone, in the dark.

Empty.

WHEN THEY FINALLY LET US OUT THE NEXT MORNING, Dew'ann wasn't there and no one spoke of her. But there was plenty of talking going on. Everyone was loud and rowdy, excited to be together after spending so much time closed up. Cam came over right away to see if I'd redo her cornrows, and Bindi's whole braid had more than fallen out. The girls who loved the TV were back in front of it, jabbering at the screen. Everyone was eager, it seemed, to get back to normal.

Only I wasn't normal anymore. But I wasn't a zombie sleepwalker in denial, either. Something had happened after that talk with the prosecutor and in the dark hours after, and I knew that I was different. I just didn't know what to do about it. But I did know I needed to give my mind a break. So I set Bindi down in front of me, started weaving her hair into another rope, and let my fingers do the work instead.

Visiting hours began. I wasn't ready to call Doug yet, and there was no one for me to see until I did. But then I heard my name.

When I saw who it was in the booth, waiting, I almost fell down.

"Bird."

She was in one of her Sunday suits. I hated knowing they'd made her take off the jacket, patted her down in places she didn't ever want to be patted. Her steel face, braving them. Just to see me.

The tears came straight to my eyes.

"You ain't the one should be crying," she said.

I cleared my throat, tried to pull myself together. For her.

"You look all right," she started. "But thinner."

I nodded. "The food's terrible." *I should be home, cooking for you*, I wanted to say, but didn't. I wanted to tell her . . . so many things. But her stiff spine was hard to approach.

"I should let you know first off," she said, all formal, "that they ain't coming around like they did. They talked to Grandma and Mel, sure, but it didn't take long for them to know we told the truth. They didn't try to find Jamelee's daddy either. That was Kenyetta just being hysteric. Of course, you being here, whatever you said—" Her eyes went over to the lady in the booth beside her.

I was clinging to my receiver like it was her arm. That Bird was no longer under investigation was like clean air or water was rushing through me. And, even better, she was here. To forgive me. Or at least start to.

"What more can I do?"

Her eyes came back, hard. "You can't do nothing."

"Bird, I—"

"I see what you're trying, writing those letters, and I came to tell you to stop. I don't—we don't—want nothing to do with you no more. I'm not saying it mean, or to give you any more trouble than you already have, but I had to come here and tell you, soon as I got them. You need to stop. You need to block us from your mind. Because that's what we have to do to you."

Everything in me wanted to plead with her, but at the same time everything knew it would do no good.

"He killed a man, Nikki."

I flinched.

"We saw on the news they arrested him, and by now I know you were in it and you were in it good. More than I even thought, and you know I told you more than once about him. That you could do better, that you needed to—"

She paused. Swallowed. Shook her head.

"Anyway, I just came here to tell you, face-to-face, straight-out, right away, that me and Jamelee, we're done with you. You send another letter, I'll tear it up, light it on fire without looking at it. Because I warned you, Nikki, and you fought me. You told me it was all right. You lied to my face and you took my car and you—"

But it was too much for her to even say. And all I could do was sit there and know it. And not be able to do anything to make it right.

"Bird, I never meant . . ."

"It don't matter what you meant. What matters is what you did. And you got to know that I've seen it and I don't want to see no more. I came here to say straight to you that I don't want to speak to you again. We had a friendship, a bond, and I'm grateful for what you did to help me and my baby, but all you've done since is break that to pieces. And I just wanted to be clear. It only seemed decent to tell you to your face."

"Bird, don't—"

But she was already standing up. Already finished with me. All I could see was her slim, strong hand putting that receiver back in the cradle. Nothing else.

"Bird," I called out, pleading. Though by then she'd already walked away, leaving only the sound of her panty hose against her skirt.

I COULDN'T EAT DURING LUNCH, BUT I TRIED TO AT LEAST follow the conversation, look involved. Concentrate on the chatter so I wouldn't have to think about Bird leaving me forever. Or any of the evil things I'd done to deserve it. I sat in the middle of all the other girls so I could pretend that there was anyone left who cared about me.

Afterward, everyone cleaned up and took their yard time. I still didn't like it out there, but Priscilla did. And though my heart shook with self-pity and sadness, though so much of me wanted to curl in a ball and shut myself away, another part of me was tired of all that. And I didn't have anything to lose anymore.

"You mind if I join you while you walk?"

Priscilla shrugged and started her fast lap around the fence. I figured that meant I could, though at first I had to work to meet her pace.

"You've been here for a while, haven't you?" I huffed eventually.

"Two weeks before you came. So, today, twenty-six days."

The short amount of time surprised me. She saw it.

"You already know how it is in here. One hour can be like a whole day. Or maybe three."

I nodded at that. "How much longer do you have?"

"They don't know."

"Because of your lawyer?"

"It's a lot of waiting. Working things out—with the family."

"Your own people?"

"Family of the kid."

I was thinking how to ask, *How old?* when she looked over at me.

"Not that you've asked, or seem to care about much more than yourself, but they say I hit this college kid on his bike. Guy pumping gas at some convenience store says he saw it. I was driving drunk, that much I know. The kid was in a coma at first, but then he died. I don't remember anything about that night. All I remember is the next day, seeing the dent in my car and thinking I must've hit a tree, feeling lucky I hadn't killed myself. It could really have been a tree, but it probably wasn't. I'd already had my license suspended from another time. So, it's more than one thing."

"Is that why you go to the meetings? After dinner?"

She nodded.

"Do they help?"

Again she shrugged. "Anything that gets you straight with yourself must help a little. Though a lot of the time it's boring. And actually feeling things sucks."

"I'm sorry I didn't ask you until now."

"Eh."

We walked awhile, quiet. I watched girls hanging out in groups in the middle of the yard, several of them shooting hoops. You could hear their shit-talking from the far end of the fence, though it was muted. Sounding more like little girls on a playground. There were other pairs of people walking laps, like me and Priscilla. One lone girl, her head shaved near bald, was doing chin-ups at one of the bars.

"Somebody died because of me, too." It felt strange to say it out loud. To be acknowledging it at all. "Not me, really. I mean, I wasn't the one with the guns. But I drove. I helped. And then I didn't tell anyone. So I might as well have shot him."

She nodded once. "That's how they see it."

"Thing is . . ." I was breathing hard, but it felt good, the blood moving in me. "I think that's how I need to see it too."

"If you want to get better, it'd help."

I snuck a glance over to see if she was being sarcastic. She wasn't.

I WAS STILL UNABLE TO SIT WITH ANY OF THE THINGS INSIDE me for very long, even though talking to Priscilla had helped. So did writing to Jamelee again later, at least until I started in on how I felt about Nicole and Dee. The last thing I wrote was *I want to punish her. It's not right, but I want to punish her almost more than I want to punish him. I want to take him away from her forever. I want to blot out the sun.* It wasn't a pleasant thing to think. And then I felt worse because I knew I could never send it.

Sunday morning there were services at eight a.m. if you wanted to go. Cam and Bindi had asked me last week to come with them, and today was the same thing. Like they were kids inviting me to a birthday party the way their eyes were all bright about it. I hadn't been to church since my grandma died and wasn't sure I wanted to start in here. Last week I just shrugged, and their smiles fell. After giving them no kind of answer again this time, I sat there, picking at powdered eggs and feeling mean. But then I started laughing at myself, thinking about church. All those mornings Bird had wanted me to come with her, me complaining it was too early. When her services weren't even until ten forty-five.

A pause came in the conversation between Cam and the girls on her other side.

"Are they real . . . preachy?" I asked.

"What, service?" Bindi piped up. "Oh no. It's nice. You sing and hear the message of the day and get to reflect. And, you know, see other people. You should really come. Just try it, at least."

I glanced at Priscilla. She was watching me, and I couldn't read what was on her face. I wasn't sure what was on mine, either. But when Bindi and Cam stood up to clear their places, along with a few other girls, I stood up too.

"Good luck," was all Priscilla said as I followed everyone out.

The "service" was in one of those rooms they used for classes on Tuesday nights. I was surprised to see a small electric piano set up. A young guy with thin brown hair and a scraggly beard stood in front of it, greeting everyone with this gentle smile. I wasn't sure what to do. The chairs were arranged in a circle, which didn't seem very churchlike to me, but there being a keyboard in here didn't seem very jail-like, either.

Cam ran right up to the piano guy, pulling me along. She gave him a big hug and introduced me to him, then to practically everyone else in the room, lots of them women not from our block. Like during my arraignment, it was strange to see women older than the rest of us, to remember that there were all kinds of folks in here. But each of them nodded at me and smiled, said they were glad to see me here. In the blur of friendliness, it took some work to remember that all of these ladies—even one who looked like she could be somebody's grandma or kindergarten teacher—were being accused of something awful enough to get them in here. And maybe a lot of them had even done it. Had put themselves, somehow, behind these bars. Just like Cam, and maybe Priscilla.

Just like me.

A fiftyish looking woman came in then, unwrapping a shawl from around her shoulders and fluffing out her very frizzy hair.

"Sorry to be late," she said in this airy way. Not like a preacher at all.

Everyone took their seats, so I did too. The woman with the shawl—she smiled and introduced herself as Anne—passed around half sheets of paper with the write-up of what we were going to do. On the back a song was written out, including the notes we were supposed to sing.

It was sort of like other services I remembered, but without as much standing up and sitting down and with much shorter prayers and not anything it seemed anyone had memorized. There was a prayer where, if you wanted to, you could ask out loud to be readied to hear the Word. After that Anne read something from the Bible: the story of Jesus and some midget tax collector hiding in a tree. She spoke some about it and—this was strange—asked our opinions. Some women had a lot to say. About being forgiving to people who were seen as oppressors or outcast for some reason. One woman talked about seeing Jesus as a real friend, somebody to invite to dinner. I didn't say anything and only barely listened, thinking instead about all my dinners with Bird and sometimes her family or friends—dinners I was never going to have again.

The keyboard finally trilled out some notes, and everyone stood up and turned their paper over to sing. I didn't know how to read music, so I was only mouthing the words. Some women in the circle had their eyes closed and were rocking back and forth, their faces raised to the ceiling. Even Bindi, who was usually pretty quiet, had a strong, clear voice. Cam's mouth smiled wide and she winked when she saw me looking at her. The piano got louder for the last verse, and so did the voices. I'd stopped even pretending to sing. Instead I just stood there, staring. Amazed at all these women, looking so free.

AFTER LUNCH, I WALKED WITH PRISCILLA AGAIN. WE DIDN'T talk a lot at first, though she did ask me about service. Mostly, I just wanted to move around. We both did. When I asked her where she got the crossword puzzles from, though, I was surprised when she told me it was her girlfriend.

She saw the look I was trying to hide on my face.

"Don't worry," she scoffed. "You're not my type."

"No, it's not that." I frowned, shocked she thought that might be what I was thinking. I had just never met a lesbian before.

"What, then? You want me to draw you a picture?"

Again, her roughness was unexpected.

"I was just thinking, it must be hard for you. Being separated from her."

This time she was the one to look surprised.

"I mean," I went on, "I was in love with somebody too—desperate love—but there's no way we can . . ." So many images of Dee blinked in my mind, some of them still making me feel breathless. And in pain. "Anyway, it's not like he's out there, waiting for me."

She nodded. "I think it's harder on her, though."

I laughed.

"No, really," she continued. "I mean, it sucks in here. It sucks not being able to do what you want, go where you want to go, live your life. It sucks everything being on total hold for you, for God knows how long. It's not *not* hard one single day. But you can put your head down about it, you know. Just put your head down and move forward, one foot in front of the other, and work through it. Day after day, you're chipping away at it."

"It's still dead boring. And the food . . ."

"Yeah, but you see how it goes. How it can go, anyway, if you're not an asshole."

I laughed again.

"But out there, in life, people are doing things. Learning things. Seeing and experiencing movies or plays or, hell, just having a bad day at work. And you're not there to talk to about it. You can't share it with them. Sure, there's letters and the phone, but it's not the same. And sometimes knowing isn't any better. It's thinking about the things I'm *not* getting to do with Lexi that'll eat me up when I let it. But then she's the one out there having to do them. Without me."

I thought of Bird, alone in the house with Jamelee and no one else, save the ones who visited. Which was plenty, but like Priscilla said, it wasn't the same as having someone there at the end of the day to talk to about all the fools you'd seen since breakfast. Someone to cook for you or help with errands. It wasn't the same as going to bed knowing there was someone else in the house. Or someone to stay up with late into the night, eating popcorn you made on the stove and watching a bad movie together just because you have to see what god-awful thing happens next.

When I went to the police, when I told them what happened, I thought I'd been thinking of Bird. And I was. But I hadn't pictured how my being gone would change things for her—not really. I hadn't thought about all the smaller, harder things she would have to face without me around. I hadn't thought—at all—that she might miss me.

It was enough, almost, to make me stop walking altogether and just sit down and cry. I'd lost Dee and I'd lost Bird too, but now it hit me how *Bird* had lost *me*. Lost me, probably, a long time ago. When Dee came back and I started hanging on every word and movement and expression of his again, undoing all of Bird's hard work after he left the first time. How I filled the house up with my chatter about him, my crying over him, bringing him in even when I knew she didn't want me to. She lost me as soon as I let him become the only thing I wanted or needed instead of seeing I might already have quite enough, right there in that house.

"Yeah," Priscilla said, seeing my face. "That whole really feeling things? I warned you that it sucks."

FIRST THING IN THE MORNING, I CALLED DOUG. I TOLD HIM
I wanted to talk about what Dee's prosecutors had requested.
He said he had court but would try to get there before dinner. I
told him to be sure to, because he was going to like what I had
to say.

While I waited for it to be afternoon, I did more hair. But
I'd gotten smart about how it worked. It was important to
have people liking you in here—for real reasons, not the ones
they'd all liked Dew'ann—but I also needed to start getting
paid.

It wasn't like I wanted anything illegal or too complicated.
Just other food, toiletries from the commissary. So far, after

braiding only three girls, I'd scored deodorant, cocoa butter lotion, two combs, and three packets of strawberry Pop-Tarts. And the braids I did weren't all that complicated. Seemed like, mostly, girls just wanted something different done.

Which I could understand now, in more than one way.

DOUG WAS ABLE TO GET A MEETING WITH ME, HIM, AND THE other two lawyers the next day. I still didn't like Hampton, but at least this time I had something to say to her.

"I want to help."

I THOUGHT AGREEING TO COOPERATE, AND TELLING Hampton my whole story (and then telling her again, into a recorder), would've made things simple, but it was a lot of waiting after that. Weeks, then months. I got a job to pass the time and keep me a little more active. Me and another girl mopped in the dining hall after everyone cleared out and two other girls swept the floors. A few others wiped the tables and loaded the dishwashers. All of them but Chelsea were nice. It wasn't fun work, but it was something to do, and we had a good enough time together. Especially at Thanksgiving, when there was a huge meal and we got to decorate. The little bits of money—twelve cents an hour—did add up eventually. It was a supplement to my doing hair, anyway, which I got better and faster at.

I wrote to Jamelee too, but I never sent any of the letters. Didn't keep them either, after a while. At first I thought the better way it made me feel, writing them, wouldn't last unless they went out in the world to her. But then Bird's voice came into my head, "We're done with you," and I'd realize there was no point. Sometimes this thought made me stop writing for days. But eventually something would happen that would make me laugh or think, and I'd be back at that notepad, scribbling. I don't know when the switch came over me—feeling good after writing even though no one but me would see it—but eventually it did. But I still wrote *Dear Jamelee* at the top of the paper.

Christmas came—presents brought in from some church group for all of us, and the guards helped us decorate a tree—and Priscilla finally got a trial date. She chewed her fingernails about down to nothing every minute after that, nervous and weary, reminding me of myself when I first got here. But I wasn't going to jump on her in the middle of the night, the way she did me. It wouldn't work, first of all, and besides, she didn't need any more scaring. Instead we walked together. Sometimes she talked. Sometimes we just went around and around. I was better at matching her stride. My legs and my lungs were getting to be almost as strong as hers.

New girls came in. Others left. They had their trials or finished their terms, and then they were out the door. Including

Bindi, who finally got her case settled out of court. Cam was really sad to see her go, so me and Priscilla had a project on our hands for a while, trying to keep her spirits up. Eventually we figured we ought to start a card game of our own since Bindi had liked that so much. Priscilla said what we were playing was Gin Rummy, but it wasn't much of any rules I'd known before, except the whole laying down sets of three. A new girl, Rae, came in, and we invited her to join us, though we had to explain the rules again to her almost every hand.

I thought of Bird plenty. Almost every day, for various reasons, and especially at the holidays. Someone would tell a story that I'd think Bird would like, or laugh just like Kenyetta used to, or there'd be something on TV I'd wonder whether she was seeing. I thought about how her business was doing, how she was getting along now without me. Who she'd gotten to help take care of Jamelee, or if maybe Jamelee was in day care now. I thought about sending her letters. Apologizing for always choosing Dee over her, for not understanding that she just wanted better for me. And sometimes I wrote them. But just like with Jamelee's, I didn't put them in the mail. No matter how bad it hurt, I knew I'd done enough to Bird. I didn't need to disrespect this last thing she'd asked of me.

AND THEN, FINALLY, HAMPTON CAME TO VISIT. IT HAD BEEN a long time since I'd seen her, and when she walked into that conference room, something about the tired look on her face gave me a flash of pity for her. It was clear how hard she working, on this case and probably others. It didn't make me like her any more, but it made me feel . . . something.

"How are you doing, Nikki?"

"Good." And then, "Thanks for asking."

"It's been a while."

"Yes, it has."

"There's a lot to wait on in a case like this."

"That's what they tell me."

We looked at each other. Both of us, maybe, a little more accepting.

"Well, while it may not seem so from your perspective, we've been progressing."

She stopped as though I should say something, but I didn't know what. I just nodded.

"And we're at a crucial point now where more of your help would be vital."

I looked at Doug. I'd told Hampton forever ago everything I knew. What more could she need from me now?

"There are still some things that aren't quite lining up. From the witness testimonies, mainly. Walking through the crime scene with one of our detectives could be very . . . instrumental."

I felt Doug looking at me. But I didn't want this decision—to go back there, to live through any minute of it—to be about my case. I had thought about Dee. Of course I had. I had thought about him and Nicole and what happened. Bird. The entire thing. But picturing any of it now didn't give me the dragged-around-and-back feeling it used to. Instead I was mad. At him, and her, and mostly myself. When Dee had wanted to get together again last May, I'd thought it meant I'd been right all along, that my love for him—our love for each other—had some *purpose*. But now I just saw what an idiot I'd been, what an idiot he obviously thought I was. Which he should have. Because

I was an idiot. I was stupid enough to let him ruin my friendship with Bird and my entire life—to help him kill someone—when he didn't even care.

But I wasn't stupid anymore. My addiction to Dee was over. And I was going to do whatever I could to keep him away from her—anyone—forever. When I first told Hampton my story, I thought I was doing it to get back at Nicole for being the one he loved. But after these long months, all of that seemed silly. Helping lock Dee up wouldn't do anything worse to her. If she'd really asked Dee to do it (I was never going to be sure; it was nothing I could prove), she had to know, being a cop's daughter, that he was going to get caught. So if she asked him to, she can't have believed they would stay together. Dee rotting in prison the rest of his life may have been part of her whole plan.

But even if it had been her idea, thinking you want somebody dead is a whole lot different from dealing with them actually being so. I'd heard enough girls talk in here to know that was true. Living without her daddy, no matter what she thought of him, was going to be punishment enough. Awful as Cherry was, bad as I wanted not to see her anymore, I didn't want her in the ground. Nicole would have to deal with her father's death, his absence, for the rest of her life. No matter whatever else she felt. And, in my opinion, that was enough.

Dee, on the other hand. He still wanted her. I knew it. He

did what he did thinking it would end with him and Nicole running off together, getting married, whatever. My helping the prosecutors get every detail down, it wasn't about her anymore. It was about teaching him a lesson. And it felt good, telling this woman who couldn't promise me any kind of deal, "I'll do whatever you need."

A COUPLE DAYS LATER I WAS GIVEN SPECIAL RELEASE TO go out to the site with Detective DuPree, the same guy who'd questioned me back in August. The one who showed up on Bird's front stoop with that search warrant. I'd forgotten he was big. Like a kid's drawing of a fat person: round from shoulders to waist, with skinny stick legs. But also—and I hadn't noticed this before—he was handsome. Smooth skin. Nice smile.

"I just need you to walk me through it," he said as we drove. I hadn't been in a car in a long time. Not one where I was allowed in the front seat. It was strange and fast—everything rushing toward us. "There are some things that don't quite line up. I'm sure, though, once you show me, it'll all become clear."

Doug had tried to insist on coming with me, but at that

point I knew he couldn't protect me anymore. I wanted to do this on my own, for my own reasons. At first, in the car with DuPree, I wondered if that had been a bad idea, not bringing Doug along. But it didn't take long for that feeling to come over me again—that feeling like DuPree and I were just talking. Over a cup of coffee. Even if there was a laptop magically rigged into the dashboard between me and him, and a staticky radio squawking from time to time.

We were driving from a different direction Dee and I had taken out there, so at first it was just a regular drive. A regular drive with a detective who needed help with investigating a murder I helped commit. It started feeling a lot less regular once we got off the interstate, though. Things started coming back to me. We turned onto roads I'd forgotten I knew. Blocks away, I guessed exactly when the brick sign for the subdivision was going to come up. I expected that cursive sign long before I saw it.

I started to sweat. Not beads and beads—more like a thin curtain over me.

"So, you came in through this entrance, right?" Detective DuPree asked.

I nodded.

He drove slowly up the hill. Turned. The houses we passed— full of neighbors. Neighbors I knew now had picked up their phones, dialed 911 when they heard the shots that day. Had looked out their windows. Seen Dee. And me. A panicky feeling rose up in me, wondering were they looking out those windows now, watching again. Would they recognize me? Come out of their houses, demanding that I pay for what had happened?

"You okay?" DuPree asked, kind.

I wiped my hands against my thighs and nodded. They'd given me sweatpants and a sweatshirt to wear out here, thinking my orange getup might raise alarm. I tried to concentrate on how much better the fuzzy fabric felt than my jail uniform.

I counted down the houses as we drew closer: four . . . three . . . two . . . one. It shouldn't have surprised me, I guess, that I would know the place before I saw it again. When I thought about August twenty-fourth, I saw Dee more than anything else. Now I was seeing the whole picture, in razor-sharp vision. The cracks in the driveway next door. The manhole cover in the middle of the road. The border of monkey grass in the yard across the street. And the house—that yellow house—with everything exactly the same, save that the plants were all gone and there was a FOR SALE sign next to the mailbox.

"She's not here?" I asked before thinking.

"Who? Miss Palmer?"

I kept staring at the house, picturing the rooms empty now. I wondered when she was here last. If she'd ever come back.

"Moved up north to be with her aunt."

"Indiana." I remembered the newscast with unreal clarity. The one we watched at Bird's, the day after it happened. I saw DuPree try to cover up being surprised I knew.

"Shame, really," he said. "Leaving town your senior year. And your daddy not there for your graduation."

I had to shut my eyes then. Hampton had shown me a picture of Deputy Palmer and his daughter, from when she was a little girl. The way they were both smiling, the way he had his arm around her, I knew he would've been so proud at her graduation. Even if she hated him. Even if she thought she wanted him dead. He would've worn a tie to the ceremony and shouted her name when she took her diploma even if there were too many people in the auditorium for her to hear. He would've put his arm around her like that again and taken her out dinner after. Somewhere fancy. He would've bought her dessert.

"You going to be able to do this?"

I opened my eyes again, forced myself to look at the house.

"What do you need me to tell you?" I said as I opened the door to get out.

I SHOWED HIM WHERE WE PARKED BIRD'S CAR, A LITTLE beyond the edge of the driveway. I told him again about the wigs, the clothes, about Dee making me put on that flannel shirt.

"That makes sense, then," DuPree said thoughtfully.

I asked him what.

"Two witnesses said they were sure a man was in the driver's seat. Which was why he asked you to bring that short wig you had. Wear that shirt."

The disguises had always felt so wrong, but something extra curled up cold in me, knowing Dee had wanted to disguise me too. Trying to confuse witnesses just that much. I shuddered.

DuPree didn't seem to notice. He asked me if I saw any shooting, and I had to tell him no, that I'd been too freaked out.

"I could hear it, though," I said, breath shuddery. DuPree and I were standing at the end of the Palmers' driveway. Six feet away from where Mr. Palmer had died. Maybe exactly in the spot where Dee had emptied out his guns.

"How many shots again?" DuPree had a little notepad out. He licked the end of his pencil like they do in old detective shows.

I imagined it, the bullets just coming and coming at Deputy Palmer. Glass bursting as they pierced through the windshield. Slamming into his body. Shot after shot. So many he couldn't move, couldn't duck down, couldn't get away. Could only raise one hand in a useless attempt to ward them off. Recognizing the hate-filled face of the boy he knew all along was bad for his daughter. And being able to only sit there, seat belt still on, and bleed.

"I'm not sure. Thirteen? Fifteen?" Tears had come to my eyes and I pushed them away with my fingertips. "It was a lot. And they came fast. I was driving away by then."

We walked down the street around the curve and went through the intersection, turned left. I showed him where I'd stopped the car, in time to see Dee running toward me between the houses.

"That lines up," DuPree said almost to himself. Then, to me, "Lady in that house over there was one of the ones who described the purple car."

I looked. It was a tan-colored house, the bottom half of it made up of those expensive-looking rocks. I was surprised she'd seen the car at all, because it was four or five houses away from where I'd picked up Dee and there were a lot of trees. She must've been standing right in front of the window when I drove by.

"He ran through here." I pointed.

DuPree nodded again, mentioned someone who saw a red-haired woman. But I wasn't focused on anything he was saying. Instead I stared down the corridor of grass between the two stately houses, looking straight into the driveway where Deputy Palmer had died. Had he still been alive when Dee took off? Had he watched Dee run, that wig flying behind him? Was there enough consciousness in him left, enough clarity, to see me there too? Struggling to take his last breaths, full of blood and pain, and me—right there—waiting to take Dee to safety?

It was too much. I dropped down to the curb and pressed my knees against my closed eyes. Tears soaked into the fabric of my sweatpants.

DuPree was nice about it. He just stood there while I cried. Waited. Didn't rush me. Probably he'd seen this kind of thing happen before. People finally getting hold of exactly what they'd done. Seeing what they'd seen in their own heads so many times, only this time, finally from the victim's side of it.

"There's nothing I can do to make it right," I said, trying

to breathe normal again. "This man's dead. His daughter has nobody, and I—"

"You're doing what you can," DuPree said over me, quiet. "You're finally doing, now, what you didn't have the strength to do then."

AS SOON AS I GOT BACK FROM THE SITE WITH DUPREE, I called Hampton. She'd said she wanted to know everything. Needed every scrap of anything that she could use against Dee. And whether it was out of remorse or guilt or anger, just plain tiredness, or revenge, I knew I had to tell her right away, before I lost my nerve.

"Hello, Nikki?"

"Hampton." I was breathing shallow, and my cheeks felt warm.

"Yes?"

"Afterward, he was laughing like a little kid. He was so excited, like he'd just won the lottery. It was what made me calm down, actually, how happy he was. Like we'd just done something good. I believed him. Do you understand what I'm saying?"

"You'll want to say all this with Doug present if this is a new addition to your testimony."

"And that's not all." This next part was going to destroy me, I knew. It would be terrible for my case, and Doug would kill me. But I had to do it. I had to tell the whole truth. "On the way home we pulled over at a rest stop and we screwed each other's brains out."

MORE WAITING. DAYS AND WEEKS OF THE ENDLESS SAME thing. Wake up, cleanup, breakfast. Mopping. Common room and doing hair. Lunch. More mopping. Outside walk with Priscilla. Cards in the afternoon. Reading time. Dinner. Mopping again. Priscilla and Cam going to their meetings. TV with everyone. Common room cleanup, count, lights-out, bed.

I wasn't hiding anymore. I'd done what I'd done. Whatever punishment came from that, I knew I deserved. Deserved because of my weak-kneed blindness, my choosing Dee over everything else. So I'd told the prosecutors everything without thinking twice. And though I was ashamed, when everything was finished, I felt cleaner than I had all year.

Priscilla got to get clean too, finally. In her own way. For days I watched her haul herself out of bed when the guards called for her earlier than regular wake-up time. She'd be gone all day at her trial. Me and Rae walked the fence outside together, talking, trying not to think of Priscilla. Cam shot hoops with the other girls. She'd gotten really good, and everyone wanted to play with her. Afterward we played cards, the three of us, sometimes with an extra girl coming into the game, filling the hole of Priscilla being gone. It wouldn't be until we were getting ready to head into dinner that she came back, not saying much.

Five days later, she was gone. The jury only discussed it for an hour. That prior DWI was apparently all they needed to convince themselves she was guilty and would likely do it again. Twelve years in prison. Fines. Community service, after.

We hardly got to say good-bye. She was only in our block about ten hours between her sentencing and getting transferred over to the prison, and half of that was count and lights-out. They came to get her at two a.m. I got to hug her and tell her I'd write, that I knew she would be okay, but it didn't feel like enough. Through the dark I watched her shuffle away, half the person she'd been when I got here.

I couldn't help but wonder if that was going to happen to me.

FINALLY WE WERE PREPARING FOR DEE'S TRIAL. IT WAS March now. Everyone told me this was quick for getting into court. It meant the case was extra important.

For a week leading up to it, Hampton and her assistant visited every day. Asking me questions, showing me my statements, going over details again and again, making sure everything was correct. Bianca worked with me for hours on just trying to maintain eye contact with her while I gave my answers. Telling me to sit up straight, showing me how to speak toward the microphone but not too close. Hampton pretended to be Dee's lawyer, firing cross-examination questions that made me squirm. Getting mad when I did.

"He's going to ask you worse," she assured me with that

unforgiving face of hers. "You're going to have to answer back strong. Stick to the story. Don't elaborate and don't get defensive. For God's sake don't mumble, and don't let anyone see that you're afraid of him. It's his *job* to make you look bad in front of the jurors. You're going to have to be stronger than this."

On our last day, Hampton told me they weren't going to let me change into street clothes when I appeared on the witness stand. I was going to have to get up there in front of everyone—including Dee—in my jail uniform.

"But I'm going to look like a *criminal*!" I wailed.

"You *are* a criminal, Nikki," Hampton growled. "At least in these jurors' eyes. You lied to the police to protect your boyfriend, you were an essential part of his scheme, and you did nothing to obstruct his plan. For over a week, you tried to help him cover it up. They are going. To think. You are. A killer. What I need you to stay focused on, what I need you to remember, is that *he* was the one who pulled the trigger. He was the one who planned this whole thing, down to the last detail. He brought you into this, and he was the one who wanted Deputy Palmer dead. This isn't your trial right now. What we're doing here, what is so vitally important, is working to prove beyond a reasonable doubt"—she had said this so many times, I was so tired of it—"that Denarius Pavon was the mastermind and executor of this plan, that he manipulated your feelings for him to get you to help, and he conducted it with motive and without remorse. If you can't be on board with that, you might as well not show up tomorrow."

I was glaring at her. Everyone told me the lawyers were supposed to be nice to you, were supposed to make you feel at ease. But Hampton could still barely stand to show me any kindness, with her brusque man voice, her unrelenting pressure.

At the same time, her strictness made me feel the way I'd felt when Priscilla's hand went over my mouth that dark night in our cell. Telling me to get something to do and quick. Something more than obsessing over my boyfriend, anyway. They both expected me to pull it together, not caring how I did it. Not praising me for it or questioning my ability. All they did was point out that I had to. Which helped me, somehow, understand that I could.

Though it was exhausting and uncomfortable—though I was so nervous, and Hampton so tough—working on this testimony was much more than just something to do, anyway. It was something to do that, if it made Dee pay for what he'd done, was going to actually be worth doing.

BUT NOTHING MARJORIE DID IN THOSE FEW DAYS BEFORE trial could really prepare me for what it was like. Early in the morning the guards got me up. Searched me, cuffed me, took me to the courthouse, and I had to wait in a holding cell there for what felt like forever. It was worse than waiting in jail, worse than those long hours in lockdown. I tried to do what Bianca told me, to go over the questions and think about the honest answers to them, to take long slow breaths and count them to a hundred if I had to, but it was hard to focus. I hadn't seen him in so long. It had been easy—easier, anyway—to quit Dee when I was completely cut off from him. When I was surrounded by jail life, by my friends. When I had no other choice. Now I wondered if it would be like it always was with Cherry. And Bo.

And Gary. And everyone else. It didn't matter how long they'd been in rehab or how many times. All it took was one sniff, one hit, one inhale, one swallow, and they were right back where they started: helpless. Hooked.

When the deputy finally came for me, I cleared my throat and breathed as calmly as I could. I tried not to be afraid. *All you have to do*, Hampton had said, *is get up there and tell the truth.*

The whole truth.

And nothing else.

WHEN THE DEPUTY SWUNG THE COURTROOM DOOR OPEN, the first thing that hit me was how many *people* were in there. Bianca had told me they'd be there, but it was still uncomfortable, walking past. I kept my eyes on Hampton and Bianca up front, hands folded before them, waiting for me to get to my seat.

As I walked to the stand, next all I could see were the faces of the jury. You wouldn't think twelve people could look like so many. All of them watching me. Judging, but trying to keep their expressions even. Hampton had told me if I looked at any of them, I'd have to make eye contact. To be relaxed. Confident, but not cocky. Respectful, but not cowed. I didn't know, at that moment, how to be any of those things. How to be anything other than what I truthfully was: afraid, ashamed, defeated, resigned.

The deputy stood in front of me and asked me to raise my right hand. Whole truth, nothing but, etc. The judge told me I could have a seat, and the deputy stepped away.

And then, there he was.

In a suit. Blue, with a pale blue shirt and a blue-and-green-striped tie. I guessed because it was his trial, they'd let him get dressed up. And he did. His gold watch was gleaming. Cuffs pulled down neat, to cover as many of the tattoos on his wrists and hands as he could. Hair freshly cut—sharp and tight. Though I couldn't smell it, I knew he was wearing cologne, and I knew it was Drakkar Noir. I'd sprayed my pillows with it once, hoping the smell of him would follow me into my dreams. That I would wake up, my nose buried in that smell as though still buried in his warm neck. I thought this, but I couldn't feel it as I looked at him. He was shaved. Clean. Skin almost radiant with freshness, though I usually liked him a couple days unshaven. Still, he seemed so loose. Even though he was sitting straight, hands folded in front of him on the table, his whole body seemed to say he had nothing to worry about. Like this was an interview for a job he knew he'd get. Easy. Confident. Not a worry in the world.

But here was the thing.

He couldn't look at me.

And it was because of this that I got through the first series of questions: basic things like my name, where I lived and worked, my age, did I know the defendant, how did we meet. Though my voice quivered and my knees were shaking—everything in me shaking, all those eyes on me, except for his—as I talked, the talking got a little bit easier. And every time I glanced at him, even though Hampton had told me not to, his eyes were focused at a spot on the table in front of him, nowhere else. Like there was a screen on its surface that was the source of the story instead of me. I told them about the fair, and our romance, and our breakup, and then last May when he came back to me. Every time I glanced, he was looking down into somewhere else. Anywhere but at the me I was now, without him.

"You were in love with him," Hampton said.

"Yes."

"*Crazy* in love with him?"

"You could say that, yes."

"So crazy that you continued to date him even though your best friend advised you against it, is that correct?"

Bird oh Bird, I'm so sorry—

"Yes."

"You wanted to be with him so badly, you didn't really question much of what he did, did you?"

Hampton had told me not to elaborate, to simply answer yes or no. "Not really."

"You gave him whatever he wanted, didn't you?"

A dangerous feeling came up in me then. A feeling that if, at that moment, he looked at me, I might falter. If he only raised his eyes for a second to acknowledge what we'd had, what we'd been— even if it was destroyed now—for just a glimmer, I might take it all back. Might fight for him again. Destroy this whole case. As Hampton went on, asking questions about our relationship, what we did together, if I'd ever met his family or his other friends, a tiny, buried part of me kept aching for the wild, borderless feeling I'd had with him. It wanted to be sucked up into the tornado of wanting him again. To lose myself—all of it—in the hot, damp satisfaction of taking whatever he dished out.

"And you never knew," Hampton said, "about Mr. Pavon's relationship with Miss Palmer, is that correct?"

For a second I looked at him. Quivered.

But he was forever blank.

"That's correct."

"Did you ever meet Miss Palmer? Or speak to her?"

"No, ma'am."

"Mr. Pavon never spoke about her?"

"He mentioned her I think once or twice when we got back together. To explain what had happened. That they had been out a few times but were broken up."

"And did he tell you why they broke up?"

"Something about her family. They didn't like him."

"Did he tell you that he was hoping to marry Nicole?"

Did I care anymore?

"No."

"You found out about their engagement later, is that correct?"

"Yes. It was when the police came to question me."

"Did you know anything about her at all?"

"No, ma'am."

"Miss Dougherty, did you have any reason to dislike Miss Palmer? To be jealous of her?"

Dee's eyes finally came up. To meet mine. And in that moment I saw a pained, pathetic face wearing an expression I was sure—it gave me chills—that Bird had seen on mine too many times. Pleading. Needing. Helpless and weak at even the mention of her, so much talk of their love. I saw that he'd never been the strong man I'd looked up to—only just less weak than I was. And now I could see that his love for her was just as blind as mine had been for him: without any sense of self. A hunger that could never get fed. Because in addiction, there is never enough. His love for her would make them both suffer. It would never make him whole.

"There's no reason to be jealous at all."

THE REST WAS GRUELING. FIRST, MY EARLY COMMENTS TO the police, brought out and shown to me, read out loud. "You lied, didn't you?" Hampton asked, looking like she wanted to rip me in half. Then the real statement, the truth—parts enough to get them away from Bird, anyway—enough to get me in jail and get Dee out of Nicole's arms. That read out loud too. But it wasn't enough. Instead Hampton made me tell the whole story again—front to back, from Friday to the end. Question after question—questions I knew were coming but were still hard to answer—guiding me further along. Making me reveal it to this room of strangers, this group of judges. To him. Every detail, every truth.

What I had done.

What he had done.

What we had done together.

The guilt was overwhelming. I'd had distance from it, knew this was what I wanted to do. I'd practiced so many times. But still, in front of all these people, it was impossible to fight. Nicole wasn't there today—Hampton said it was too difficult for her—but I knew some of her family were. And knowing this, all of Hampton's questions were made ten times worse. *Why didn't you drive away? Why didn't you make him drive his own car? Why didn't you go to the police? Why did you lie?* The shame, the wonder at my own stupid willingness flooded over me, seeing all over again how they saw it. Saw me for the pathetic fool I was. I wanted to stop everything, lean in, say a hundred times, *I'm sorry. Don't you see I'm sorry?* but it was like Hampton could sense me weakening. Each time I hesitated, she came firing in with one more hard question, pushing me forward. Propping me up.

"You have your own trial coming up involving this case, don't you, Miss Dougherty?"

The mention of it made me even more nervous. And I was shaken. Spent. "Yes."

"And this testimony can be used against you in that trial, is that correct?"

"Yes."

"You are also aware that if it's revealed that you've perjured yourself in any way during this testimony, the results could be very grave for you."

Tears now. "Yes."

"So what you're telling us today is the truth, is that correct?"

Shudder. "Yes."

"The whole truth."

"*Yes.*"

"And you're giving this testimony without any promise from me, is that correct?"

"Yes."

Her voice meaner, harder—a diamond. "We have made no exchange whatsoever for your cooperation, is that right?"

"Yes."

"But you're still hoping that the court will be lenient with you."

"I—"

"Answer the question, Miss Dougherty. You hope that, when it comes time for your own trial, the court will have mercy."

"Of course." Wiping my eyes. "I mean, *yes.*"

"That is all, your honor."

AFTER THAT, ALL I HAD TO DO WAS STAND IT THROUGH THE cross-examination. Hampton'd warned me Dee's lawyer would try to make me look bad, and he did, but after already baring everything like that, I didn't much care. I had already been stripped down. Everybody already knew what I was. And besides, most of the questions he asked—wasn't this really my idea, hadn't I been enraged with jealousy, didn't I make Dee do drugs—I could honestly answer no to.

He was finished with me before I expected. And, like that, it was over. The judge was telling me I could go. I stood up, afraid for a second I wouldn't be able to, but then I found my legs and began to walk.

I didn't even look at Dee. I didn't need to. Instead I focused on Hampton as I passed by. The files all over the table, and what she needed next, took most of her concentration, but she did look up. It wasn't a smile she gave me, exactly, but I knew enough about her and what I'd just done to see that she was proud.

DOUG CALLED ME EVERY DAY AFTER THAT TO TELL ME HOW the case was going. It took three more days to deliver all the evidence. "The judge likes to take a lot of breaks," he explained. "The going is slow."

But even after the case was finished, there was more agonizing waiting. Doug expected the jury to make a quick verdict, but instead they deliberated for two whole days. He phoned after each time they came in with a question, and each time his voice was just as tight and anxious as I felt. Doug had decided we'd wait until Dee's trial was over before we thought about changing my plea. And maybe we could. But whatever was happening in there, it was going to affect me too, in more ways than one. I could hear the doubt chipping away at Doug the same way it was me. If the jury was unsure whether Dee really did it, what was going to happen? Would all of this—the whole horrible thing—come to nothing? Would he walk free, just like that? I had been doing this for myself, yes, and for Bird and the people Dee had hurt, but I'd also done it to show him he wasn't as all-powerful as he thought. I'd done it to correct a wrong. So if the jury didn't back me up? What the hell was I supposed to learn from that?

The last call came on a Thursday. We'd just had commissary stuff delivered, and I'd gotten a fresh, clean notepad.

Someone called from the guard booth: "Phone call, Dougherty."

I was surprised to hear Hampton's voice on the line: wet and trembling. "Nikki?"

My entire body went cold at the sound of her. Numb. "We didn't get it, did we?"

She cleared her throat. Almost a little girl sound. "They convicted him, Nikki. Denarius Pavon was found guilty."

I slid to the floor and wept with relief.

They gave him life plus twenty. There'd be an appeal, Hampton said. It could be another year, two, before he really started his sentence, and I might have to testify again. There was still my own trial to finally focus on now too. But I knew we'd done it. I knew without a doubt, no matter how long it took, that Dee was finished. Even if he got off for good behavior one day—even if he never felt sorry for what he'd done—he had no more power over me. He could peacock it around prison all he wanted. Outside of it, even. But he would know and I would know and every person in that courtroom would know that he'd thought he was a god. And this girl he'd treated like dirt—this girl he'd tossed around like a toy he didn't even want—had helped bring him back down to earth.

THE DAY AFTER DEE'S VERDICT, I GOT A NEW CELL MATE, Maude. I spent the next few days showing her the ropes, introducing her to people, learning her story. Priscilla would laugh if she saw it—me, some kind of leader—and it made me miss her.

I was in the common room doing Maude's hair. We were both talking to Cam, who was getting amped up about her own trial, when one of the guards hollered, "Dougherty, you got a visitor."

I hadn't had a visitor in I didn't know how long. Not outside of the lawyers. Cherry could be in jail herself for all I knew, and Gary still had a lot more time to serve. There was no one left outside who wanted to see me. I'd come to grips with that months ago. Had Dee's mom come to scream curses? Was it one of his friends, vowing revenge?

But as soon as I saw her waiting in the visitor's booth, all these thoughts melted behind me. My face collapsed into whatever it does when you feel—all over—a grateful and honest love.

"Bird."

She was dressed up again, like for church, and she had Jamelee on her lap. She smiled, and it was the warmest, most spreading thing over me.

"We saw on the news. Congratulations, I guess."

"Thanks."

Jamelee was grabbing for the cord of Bird's phone. Bird had to bobble a bit to get her out of the way.

"She's bigger," I said. "Getting to be like a real little girl."

"She's fat is what she is, but that's what you want on a baby, so."

I had so much to say, so much to ask. But I had so much to listen for, too.

"Thank you for coming," I started. "It's good to see you."

She smiled again, this time shyer. "I thought a lot about what I would say to you."

"I've thought about you too. Every day."

Her face darkened just a bit. I'd already said too much.

"Do you know what's going to happen next?" she asked.

"No," I told her, honest. "My own trial, I guess, and then . . ." I shrugged.

"Are you scared?"

I looked at her. "I was. And maybe I will be again. But I'm not right now."

"You told them the whole thing, didn't you? I mean . . ." Her eyebrows went down as she tried to find the words. "They're putting him away because of what you said?"

"It wasn't just me. The lawyers worked really hard on the case. The police. Detective DuPree. Everyone. But I know my testimony helped."

She nodded at that.

"I'm proud of you," she said, soft.

All the tears I still hadn't cried for her came pouring out. I bowed my head, not wanting her to see. Not because I was ashamed, but because she'd already borne so much. And it was my turn to bear some things for her.

"I'm so sorry, Bird," I was finally able to say.

"I know you are."

"And I miss you and Jamelee, and Kenyetta and everybody. I wish you knew me now, the way I am. I would be a real friend to you, Bird. So much better than before. I wish I could meet you all over again and we could—"

But she stopped me, shaking her head. "Things can't go

back the way they were, Nikki. Not you and me. Not like that."

She looked away.

"There's a feeling in me for you that's just . . . broken. I've prayed about it nearly every Sunday, knowing I should forgive you. I do feel sorry for you, and I know in large part you couldn't help it, but there's just something . . . wrong in me now about the whole thing. And about you. I'm proud, and I hope things will be better for you now. But you and me . . ."

Tears dripped onto my chin when I shook my head. "I really messed things up."

She didn't say anything. Her face was sorry, but firm.

I sucked in a deep breath, tried to wipe my face. "Well, can I write you? Sometime? Tell you how things are going?"

She looked at Jamelee. "You can write."

"Okay." I sighed. "I will, then."

I didn't want her to go. I didn't want her to walk away with my face full of tears and this strangeness between us being the last thing we might remember of each other, so I asked her how she was. I asked her to tell me about work, our friends, and the things Jamelee had learned how to do. I could see, at first, it was hard for her, trying to talk like things were normal. Like this was a friendly visit. I could see she didn't want me to think, just because she was telling me about getting promoted to assistant manager at KFC and that she was thinking about hiring some inexpensive college kid to help her with the bookkeeping part of her dress work, that things were better between us. I could see she didn't want me to mistake this kindness on her part for anything more than that. And I tried to show her—asking her but not asking too much—that I really understood.

We talked for the entire half hour the guards allowed, and it went far too fast.

"I guess we gotta go," she said, smoothing down Jamelee's dress and straightening herself up.

"I'm glad you came." New tears were pricking. "It means a lot to me."

"You're not a bad person," she said, her eyes meeting mine. "You never were."

"Just one who made a lot of bad mistakes." My voice was half laugh, half cry.

"And is working to fix them."

"Trying." But I was getting too shuddery, thinking of her leaving me. And maybe never coming back.

She stood up, keeping the receiver tucked under her chin while she balanced Jamelee. "Say bye-bye, little girl."

Jamelee looked at me, big, round eyes in a big, round face. Darling bow mouth like something on the best present you would ever get.

"Bah-bah." She smiled, very proud of herself.

Bird smiled too. At her daughter, then at me.

"Take care of yourself, Nikki."

I managed to smile a little back. "It's all there's left for me to do."

A WEEK OR SO LATER, DOUG CAME TO SEE ME, ALL IN A flurry.

"They want to settle," he said, unable to conceal his glee. He slid some papers across the table between us. "In my opinion, it's because of his appeals and the amount of resources this case is already taking, but it's also clearly because of your cooperation."

The world was rushing around me. I wouldn't have to go on trial? It was almost—all of it—truly over? "I don't understand."

"They're asking for more time than I think you should have to do at all, considering the time you've served already, but it's relatively fair. I don't want to rush you because there's a lot to think about here on both sides—the pros and the cons—but, Nikki, this could really be a golden ticket for you. If you decided to take it."

I looked at the papers in front of me. I would have to go down to the law library, try to get one of the women who hung out there to explain everything to me—even after I heard all of what Doug had to say. It would cost me an elaborate hairdo, maybe a few other things, but I knew I could get help in wrapping my head around it.

"Gimme a day or two," I told him. "I'll call you."

DOUG AND I BOTH PROBABLY KNEW I WAS GOING TO accept their offer. I just wanted a little more time for the shock to wear off and a chance to talk to my friends. Cam was elated and told me to take it immediately. I'd already been through one trial, she pointed out. Rae also thought I should avoid court altogether, if for no other reason than to not have to wait around here for another stretch of forever.

The day of my sentencing, I didn't know how to feel. After Dee's verdict, I'd finally been able to let go of this giant rock I'd been carrying around. I hardly knew how to stand up, move my arms, walk around without that weight on me. My brain didn't know how not to have his trial on my mind. It was freeing, but it was also strange. I had, once again, thought only about him. My own trial had disappeared behind his.

Now, maybe not having to go through my own trial either, another weight was lifted. One I'd gotten so used to, I didn't even know I'd been carrying it. Without it holding me down, I thought I might just lift off the ground, float out into space. It was a happy feeling, but a scary one too. Who was I going to be out there, when I was rid of Dee and truly done with being the girl I was with him?

Standing next to Doug, facing the judge, my insides were liquid.

The judge spoke. Such a heavy weight: "Nicola Dougherty, after consideration of your case and your voluntary cooperation with the state in the case against Mr. Denarius Pavon, for the crimes against which you have been charged, you are hereby sentenced to a continued eighteen months at the county jail, followed by three years of probation, during which you will also perform community service."

There was more. Doug said something. The judge said something else. I said a few things too. But it was over quickly. We stood. The judge left the room and then it was Doug hugging me and me hugging him and my entire spirit floating, floating, floating off into I didn't know where. I didn't know what was going to happen next. I didn't know quite how I was going to get through another year and a half of jail, and I didn't know how I was going to feel or where I was going to go whenever I got out. Cherry's, I guessed, at first, but I wouldn't stay there ever again. Maybe I would try to find Bindi. Visit Priscilla. Get my old job back. Or find a new salon and start again from scratch. Maybe I'd get an apartment and my own car, and maybe—just maybe, after enough time—I'd find a way to go back to Bird, to rebuild the friendship I'd shattered. There was so much whirling in me, so much I didn't know. There was so much to think about, and try, and discover.

One thing I did know, and I knew it deep in my core. As we left the courtroom—Doug clapping me again on the back—I knew wherever I went, whatever happened next, I was finally, truly going to be free.

ACKNOWLEDGMENTS

As always, with a book, there are so many people to thank. For this one, I must first acknowledge those who helped me get all the details straight: Jill Polster, Jeanne Canavan, Jan Hankins, Ingrid McGauhey, Karlyn Skall, Jennifer Mann, Muffy Blue, and Will Price of Muckraker—thanks for your honesty and your generous support.

Next up, as per usual, my editor, Anica Rissi, deserves a ton of thanks, mainly for believing in this project. I will never forget the Brooklyn Bridge walk wherein I told you this whole story and we figured out what this book should be. Thanks for all the encouragement and enthusiasm ever since then.

Scott, you deserve my thanks every day. But in this case, if for no other reason than helping me get through that terrible February that was the inspiration for this entire thing.

The team at Simon Pulse always earns my gratitude, and this time is no exception. Thanks to *all* of you for making this a reality!

Lastly, I want to thank all of my readers and enthusiasts. To every blogger, every librarian, every fellow author, every teacher, every reader, every bookseller, and every individual person who ever picked up a book of mine and felt it might be worth examining beyond the cover—thank you so unbelievably much. I can have no career, can do nothing in this writing life, without you, and there would be no new book, no new endeavor of mine, without you there supporting it.

TERRA ELAN McVOY is the author of *Pure, After the Kiss, The Summer of Firsts and Lasts,* and *Being Friends with Boys.* She has had many jobs (and degrees) that center around reading and writing, from managing an independent children's bookstore to teaching writing classes, and even answering fan mail for Captain Underpants. Terra lives and works in the same Atlanta neighborhood where many of her books are set. To learn more about Terra's life visit terraelan.com.

Don't miss this sneak peek of

TERRA ELAN McVOY

AUTHOR OF *THE SUMMER OF FIRSTS AND LASTS*

in deep

How much are you willing to lose to win?

GRIER AND I ARE FLOATING IN HER GLOSSY, TURQUOISE
pool, both of us in separate inner tubes, pushing each other
around with our feet and staring at the dark, humid sky when
she goes, "Dare me to do something."

I raise my head to look at her. Sure, she had suck times at the
meet today, and pizza with the team afterward is always a Michael
Phelps–praising bore, but we haven't played Dare in a while.
Mainly because at this point we can't think of anything we haven't
already done that isn't completely disgusting, would require too
much pain-in-the-ass planning or equipment, or would end up
with one of us getting seriously hurt or arrested. That I got tired of
her chickening out one too many times was part of it too, which is
why I'm surprised now. And, I'm out of practice.

"Uh—I dare you to pretend you're in love with Shyrah for a
week."

She groans. "Way too easy."

Which is true. If one of the other girls in the club even looks at Shyrah for too long at practice, he's sneaking up to me later, asking me should he ask her out.

"Okay. I dare you to . . ." I look around, trying to find something. We already climbed on top of the cabana once, to see if we could jump from there into the pool, but the distance really is too far. "I dare you to lick Peebo's butthole."

She grins and starts whistling for her dog.

"Sick." I splash her. "I was just kidding. He's inside, anyway."

"Here," she says, slipping free of her tube. I watch her slide underwater to the ladder, where she climbs out, tugging the edges of her bikini away from her narrow butt. I've seen Grier's body a thousand times, but it doesn't make her elfish perfectness any less obvious. Other girls on the team are jealous, I guess. Maybe I would be too if she weren't so slow in the water. She even looks good with her head shaved now, after I *Jackass*ed her with a pair of clippers last month and took a huge hunk right out of her dark, glossy locks. Her mom was plenty pissed, but even Grier thought it was funny, and now she just looks sexier. More tough.

She moseys over to the cabana and starts rummaging behind the bar. I don't really feel like drinking tonight, but at Grier's it's always around. Daring her to drink some kind of crazy mixed-up shot isn't much of a dare anymore either, but maybe this will make her less pissy or whatever it is she's been lately.

Not that Grier is that complicated. I met her when I left my high school team to join our more challenging private swim club at the end of ninth grade. Grier's a sprinter (I'm long-distance), and she'd already been a member of the club for two years, so she seemed dedicated, like me. Over time, though, she revealed herself to be the kind of girl I didn't think existed in real life. That gorgeous rich girl with an absent, globe-trotting father and a pill-addled, socialite mother; the girl who gets to spend three hundred dollars at Whole Foods on her parents' credit card over the weekend because that's easier than either of them having to figure out how to actually take care of her. She's that girl who vacations in Bali or the cliffs of Iceland or some other no-high-schooler-really-visits-there place. She goes to the best private school in Atlanta, and still her parents are constantly talking about sending her to London because they don't think she's getting an adequate education here. (Grier says they just want her out of their hair once and for all, but she'd still love to go.) She swims, mainly, so she can gorge on gourmet pizzas, organic hamburgers, bottomless margaritas, and expensive desserts. In middle school, whenever I read books that had characters like Grier in them, I'd say, "Nobody's life is really like that." But that was back when I actually read books. That was before I met Grier.

At first, when she started inviting me over, I thought she was just being nice. It took only two sleepovers though to understand that a rich, pretty girl like her doesn't have to be nice to a scrappy, Salvation Army latchkey kid like me. Instead Grier thought I was funny. Different. She told me once that I'm the only other person who hates people more than she does. And if it works for her, I'm not going to argue.

Now I spend pretty much every weekend over at her place. For me, Grier's the only one in the club who comes close to having a sense of humor or rebellion. Besides, being at her place means I don't have to hang out with Mom and my stepdad, Louis, either. Plus there's the cushy environs and excellent chow. Though Grier and I do the normal things that girls do together—complain, gossip, paint our toenails—we also spend a lot of time watching human stunt videos, which is where Dare came from. I thought I was the only one who was obsessed with "People Are Awesome," and *Jackass*, until I commented under my breath about it at practice, and Grier's eyes lit up like a Christmas tree on fire. We've filled a lot of our weekends with trying to invent stunts of our own—I'm still working on the four-inch-nail-in-the-nose trick—but for the last few weekends, because of what, I don't know exactly, we just watch the videos. And even then she seems bored.

Tonight though, we're apparently back to more than watching. When Grier comes over to sit on the edge of the pool, she's holding a round container.

"Dare me to snort this salt."

Meaning the margarita salt in her hand.

"That shit's hard little crystals. It'll hurt like hell."

"Yeah, but don't you want to see what happens? There's a sugar rimmer in there too. I'll dare you to do that after."

I don't much want to snort anything, since enough water goes up my nose on a daily basis, but Grier's going to do it whether I dare her or not, and then she'll just call me chicken all night for not making it official. I know. I've done it to her.

"Okay, fine. I dare you to snort that salt."

She takes off the lid and stares into the plastic dish for a moment, and then puts a couple of pinches in a thin line on her wrist. I paddle closer, wanting to see what happens. She waits a beat, holds her wrist up to her nose, and then, whiff, the white line disappears.

"Shit," she says, coughing.

When she looks up, there's blood pouring out her nose.

"Shit," I say back. "Are you okay?"

She coughs again, slightly gagging. "Stings like a bastard."

"Jesus. Let me get you a towel."

I climb out of the water and grab a bath sheet that probably costs more than all the cheap, secondhand furniture in my room combined.

"Wait. Check it out." She points into the pool. Drops of her blood are spiraling and unfurling in the water like devilish smoke. We stare at the blood for what feels like five minutes.

Long enough so that the red forms more of a cloud than wisps.

"You need some ice on that." I hand her the towel and stand up for the house.

"Hold up." She leans back toward the lounge chair behind her, reaching for her shorts and her phone. "Take my picture first."

Her chin, throat, and chest are now dripping blood.

"You're not going to post this."

"Why not?" She grins. "At least then we'll have proof something happened, for once. Don't be so boring."

That's a dumb thing to do out of boredom, I almost say. But it'd sound defensive. I need to get her cleaned up anyway, because apparently I'm snorting that sugar next. It's not like I can let Grier win.

SUNDAY'S ALWAYS THE LOWEST POINT OF MY WEEK. Though sleeping in is great, a day without practice feels a little unhinged, no matter what else is happening. Grier and I usually make breakfast, but once she drops me off at home, it's impossible to avoid Louis and Mom. I end up doing yard work, laundry, or washing the car. Regular- kid chore kind of things. Sometimes we go on errands. Or else I just watch TV. Make myself stuff to eat. Go online, flip through a magazine, or do enough of my homework to keep up the club's required GPA, which you'd pretty much have to be in a coma not to get.

The second half of Sunday though—that's when we go to the cemetery.

My real dad was a firefighter. But he got killed in an accident when I was ten. Lightning hit this elementary school, and a fire started on the roof while some of the administrators were inside, having a work retreat to discuss plans for the new year. The fire spread fast because of the old insulation, plus all the papers in storage. Almost everyone got out, but there were two people in the library who got stuck by a fallen shelf. My dad and two of his friends rushed in. They got the people out, but then Dad went back for a final check. That's when part of the roof caved in.

They're pretty sure he died right away. That's what my mom told me, anyway. Otherwise he would've lain there, pinned and hurt, feeling the flames close in. I believed her then, and I guess I still do.

I don't remember a lot of the next year. Mom doesn't either, except that I had a lot of nightmares and had trouble getting to sleep at night. We had to move into an apartment. Not a nice one either. I came home from school and stayed there by myself for a few hours until Mom got off of work. Wives of the other guys at the station brought us food for months, which people do when someone dies, I guess, but eventually I realized we wouldn't have eaten at all if they hadn't. I'm not sure what I did with myself when I was on my own. Probably read a lot of books.

Then there was seventh grade, and I must've gotten better

because I did have some friends. I got really into scribbling mean parodies of dramas that would happen at school for them, making us all laugh. I guess I was all right.

And then Mom and Louis met at one of their company Christmas parties. They don't work on the same floor or even in the same department, so they hadn't seen each other before, but they didn't waste a lot of time making up for that. We moved again—this time into Louis's house—and I was suddenly in a different school. There was a pool within walking distance. Mom told me I was starting swimming lessons, something we wouldn't have been able to afford even when Dad was alive. It'd get me out of the house, she said. Maybe I could make new friends.

We didn't start going to the cemetery every Sunday until about a year ago. Mom couldn't handle it before, I guess. Or didn't think I could. Maybe she thought Louis would feel strange about it. But on top of being gung ho about becoming the stepdad-slash-swim-cheerleader to the sullen, quiet daughter of a bloated, wrung-out widow, Louis was all on board for making special family time to go visit my dad's grave. I think the whole thing might've even been his idea.

Now my mom has gone gangbusters with it. It's like she's got to show off to Louis how much she cares. Nearly every week we bring something different—fresh flowers or a replacement for the plastic ones she has there in pots. Photos of my dad in cheap frames. Letters that she writes to him about me. Pumpkins at Halloween or poinsettias at Christmastime. I only go because they make me. I go because I don't have a choice. But I knew a long time ago that my father wasn't in that hole. When he first died, it felt like maybe his energy was still hovering there, but now when we visit, there's nothing. Just his strong, handsome face in those old, fading photos. My father's not anywhere anymore. Except in whatever scraps that managed to stay distinct after his DNA got all mixed up with Mom's to make me.

TIMOTHY BURRELL POLONOWSKI. BELOVED SON, HUSBAND, AND FATHER. SEPT. 1973–AUG. 2008 the tombstone reads. It always bothers me that he never got to his thirty-fifth birthday. But mainly during our weekly visits I look around at the other graves, the paling flower arrangements. It's quiet here. That is, until another car moves down one of the long drives, and another family gets out to stand over a piece of grass and a chunk of stone.

Today my mom's actually crying. I clench my quads tight, and squeeze my rib cage toward my bellybutton a few times. Try to exhale in one long stream. Who knows what's gotten into her. Maybe it's because summer's almost here. Though still it's three months or something until the anniversary. It's like the cemetery visits have made Mom more goopily nostalgic than she was when he died. Then, she was just—blank. Weak and exhausted all the time, like everything had gotten sucked out of her. There was nothing I could do. Until Louis came along.

"I'm grateful to him," Louis murmurs, rubbing Mom's shoulders. "Every day."

He would squash you, I think. But Louis is being nice. He's taking care of us. Trying to.

So I stand there, arms down by my sides, counting breaths. Eventually we leave. I don't say good-bye, though Mom does, every time.

MONDAY MORNING, AS SOON AS THE ALARM BEEPS FROM my bedside table, my mind is up, knowing what I need to do, mentally packing snacks, and pulling on my clothes—but I let myself lie there for another ten seconds. Thirty. The idea of thirty more is often tempting, but then the training kicks in and I sit up, put my feet on the floor. Thanks to days and weeks and months of this, it doesn't take much to push myself up and through the steps. Bathroom. Pee. Pajamas off. Pull on any kind of clothes—usually cutoff sweatpants and a long-sleeve T-shirt. Make bed, pound pillow. Accept banana and protein bar from Louis, who is drinking his first cup of coffee. Eat. Pull on ball cap hanging by the door. Grab gear bag as we go out into the garage to get in the car, head to school.

I used to complain, like everybody else. I used to moan. When I first started swimming, I hated it. Hated Louis, in particular, for being so peppy about the whole thing, excited to connect with his new stepdaughter, since he'd never been married and had no kids of his own. The swimming thing was just a random project I guess they both picked for me. But then, sometime in the fall of eighth grade, it became clear to me and everyone else that I was actually good. I could go faster than half my team without even trying. I made Junior Cut before anyone expected.

Somewhere in there I stopped complaining and started appreciating how tough I was getting, how lean and strong I was compared to everyone else. I went through puberty like normal, sure, but with all my swimming, everything on me stayed hard and flat. Other girls started getting boobs and hips, but I was shaped more like a two-by-four than a tart. And the weird thing was, it didn't bother me. It was like my body could do this thing that nobody else's could. I was strong and I was fast. I could hold my breath longer than anyone I knew.

I was also reading and watching a lot of interviews at that time—it's stupid to talk about Lochte or Phelps, but it's stupider not to pay attention to winners like that—and they kept echoing what Van was trying to teach me: That to really succeed, you have to not think about winning or losing. You have to think about nothing at all and just swim. And so then I got this idea in my head to see what, exactly, this body of mine could really do if I got my mind fully out of the way and disciplined myself to do just that. How fast I could go. How far I could swim. How unbeatable I could be.

There were a series of tricks and things I had to use at first, games I'd play with my brain and ways I'd secretly reward or punish myself, but eventually they worked. Now, no matter how tired I am, no matter what's going on, or how tempting another few minutes of sleep might seem, once I get myself up and started, it's like my body just knows what to do.

The best thing is, it always works.

I can't say the same thing for Louis. Unlike me, he needs about three cups of coffee and some kind of sugary carbohydrate before he can function, and every morning it's like he's dragging himself out of the house at 6:45 for the first time. When I get down to the kitchen, he's leaning against the counter and staring into his cup like he can't remember why it's there.

"Louis?"

"Mmph?" Bags under his eyes. Paunch over his belt.

"You ready?" I'm laughing at him. He knows it.

"How many more weeks of this?"

"Five. And then we get to start summer practice." I clap my hands cheerleader-style.

"It's an hour later than all this noise, at least."

I pat him on the shoulder and give him a little shove toward the garage door.

. . . .

It's not that he's not into my swimming. Once I joined the club, Louis was more serious about it than I was in some ways. He even changed his work schedule around so he can take me to school, go into work, and then leave an hour earlier than everyone else to take me to practice. The day after my sixteenth birthday, Louis took me for my driver's test, just for safety's sake, but even though we're better off now, we still can't afford another car. This deal works out okay. That there's a Dunkin' Donuts between my school and his office is an added bonus for him, but he really does care. And I know it.

We leave our neighborhood, the radio droning classic rock, though the volume's barely up. As we pull onto Monroe, I point to a dusty maroon station wagon with a low-hanging back end.

"On his way home from a janitorial shift at one of the office complexes downtown."

This is our game. A way to not just sit in the car silently focused on how tired we are or feel like we have to talk about anything else, either. I started it my first summer practice with the club as one of the ways to trick myself. Louis still enjoys it, even during the school year. It's another thing that's comfortingly automatic about my life: playing this game with Louis every morning instead of anything else.

"Which complex downtown?"

"Um . . ." I try to remember any names.

Louis makes the sound of a buzzer and slaps the meaty heel of his hand on the steering wheel, the coffee kicking in. "Too slow, too slow. What about her?"

We're passing the gas station that's a famous hangout for hookers and drug deals.

I make the buzzer noise myself. "Too easy."

"Okay, this guy."

And like that, all the way to school.

THAT I DON'T CARE MUCH ABOUT SCHOOL IS AN understatement. But it isn't because I'm so absorbed in my swimming. (Though that is a mighty convenient justification, for many teachers.) Instead it's the senseless, mind-numbingness of the whole situation. The timed bells. The shuffling to the lockers. The disgusting cafeteria. The way we're all supposed to be so excited about cheerleading and baseball scores and yearbook and all that. People say sixteen is the best year of your life—they make such a stupid deal of it. But sixteen? The pinnacle? Not for me, thanks. Of course it's true that even the best swimmers have pretty short careers, but that's why I'm looking for a swim scholarship to a decent college, away from here. It's not like I haven't thought this through. Whether my high school peers know it or not, there needs to be something beyond all this, and for me swimming's the way I'm going to get it.

Maybe it's the classes I'm in—why school mostly sucks. Maybe in AP and IB and Advanced Gifted Superfantastic Film Studies it's all academic overabundant enthusiasm all the time. But I wouldn't know. A lot of the other club members are hard-core students. They do nothing but swim and homework. They obsess about their GPAs, their academic standing, and being in the tenth percentile. Eight hours of sleep a day, and all that. But when I decided to stop thinking and just swim, school fell under the no-thinking umbrella, too. I just didn't see the point. Not here. Not in this place, with its cookie-cutter conversation and overworked, underpaid teachers tiredly reigning over classrooms full of kids whose parents call to hassle them if their precious baby gets less than a B+.

So I don't get to talk about *The Great Gatsby* with Mrs. Bowles and all the lit heads. I don't frown over string theory in Advanced Physics II or whatever, and I don't get to solve the math problems of the universe in Quadruple Trig 1000. Instead I'm as basic as they get: regular English (Mrs. Drummond, who thinks that twenty-first-century high school students are still interested in Newbery Medal–winners from 1964); PE (ha), Math for Dummies (really it's Algebra II with Dr. Herrington, who was cool about it when he failed me last year, and let me take it again instead of doing summer school); Spanish II (easy, because Señora Gupta is half-blind); Enviro Science (with Ms. Chu, who's actually pretty cool); and the one semi-interesting class, Dr. Woodham's U.S. Conflicts, which is just one of the many alterna-history courses this school is famous for offering.

As long as I make it through without fucking up enough to get me thrown out of the club, and as long as I nail National Cut at State next month, it doesn't matter. It's not that I don't want to learn something halfway useful or interesting. It's just that I know I can't do it here. So I get up early and walk through my classes. I don't make myself a disciplinary problem, but I don't really make an effort, either. When the bell rings at the end of the day, I walk out the door and take myself to the pool, which is where I'll earn my way to something better, pretty much anywhere I want.

Having Charlie with me at school has helped—at least, lately. We met on the school team at the start of freshman year and became team pals right away. We rolled our eyes together behind the coach's back, joked around. Buddies, whatever. But I didn't stay on that team long, because, honestly, the team sucks, and I'd heard about the club, which was way more vigorous. Charlie had a girlfriend on the team, this girl Sarah. They were pretty inseparable. After I quit, I didn't see much of him, even though he lives just a couple blocks away. I didn't even know he and Sarah had broken up until Coach Brubeck asked me to go to a meet with them at UGA last month, just to help up their scores and times. On the bus back, tired and pizza-drowsy, Charlie told me all about it—how serious Sarah'd gotten, talking about the future all the time. He said he missed me being around, that the team wasn't the same since I'd left. And I ended up kissing him. I don't know. He's good-looking and funny. A relationship-relationship isn't anything I have time for or interest in, but having someone to get it on with is way better than not, and plus, the extra tiredness helps me sleep better than I have in months.

Today at lunch he's at our table before I am, and as soon as I walk into the cafeteria, he smiles and raises one hand in greeting. I go over, drop my bag in my chair, and head straight for the rack of still-warm plates at the end of the salad bar. Following me in line, he rubs the tight spot between my shoulder blades, but I roll myself out from under his hand, pretending I'm stretching.

"You okay?" I can sense, just by the tone of his voice, that his dark eyebrows are scrunched down.

"I just don't understand why every teacher has to give us a fucking progress report today. PE? Are you serious? Do I care that I have a C in that class? Absolutely not, Coach Bradley. Not in the slightest."

I'm practically flinging banana peppers onto my plate. And, screw—most of the spinach is wet and wilted.

"Month of school left," he says. "Some people want to know."

"Yeah, well, I don't. Just gimme my 2.75 and let me get out of here."

"You worried about Conflicts?"

I ignore him, continuing down the salad bar to the black olives and the feta, mounding my salad high and dousing everything with plenty of oil and vinegar.

"I'm sure it's not as bad as you think," he tries again when we're back at our chairs. "And if it really is, you still have time. The exam's the main thing."

Charlie took U.S. Conflicts last year. This year he's on to Modern Presidential Campaign Strategies or some crap like that. The AP version, I think. If they have that.

"Woodham's not the extra-credit type," I remind him. I know. I asked about it when my third D shook a bit of my confidence about gliding through this class like the others. *Why would I give you extra,* Ms. Polonowski, he'd said, *when it's apparent you're barely interested in getting any credit at all?* Pompous prickmouth.

Charlie chomps a forkful of red cabbage. There's a glaze of French dressing along the right hump of his upper lip. He talks around it. "Maybe I can help."

"You'll really give me your tests from last year?" I feel halfway hopeful.

He fake-glowers at me. "No. But I can look at yours, give you some pointers, and let you know what to focus on for the next three weeks."

"Jerk."

He pauses, about to put another bunch of cabbage into his mouth, still amused. "You're gonna have to learn sometime, Ivy League."

"You know I don't care about Ivy League."

"Sure you don't."

He's teasing, but it's stupid.

"You may think that the National Merit Scholar Jerkoff Program sounds like fun," I say, "but I'm not interested in spending four years pretending I care about the Pythagorean philosopher's pee hole. Or even discovering nuclear fusion. It just needs to be something besides some Podunk community college around here, is all. I'm not going to turn into my mom."

"Whoa, okay."

I stab my salad. Charlie waits. When he starts up again, instead of being snarky or impatient, he's calm and almost sweet. "No matter where your swimming takes you, you're eventually going to have to study, Polo. Woodham's good practice. And you like that class."

"Woodham's a good asshole is what."

"All you have to do is pass the exam, Brynn. It's not that big a deal."

"I know," I grumble.

"You won't have to go to summer school. Your training will be fine."

I spear the olives and peppers on my plate. I know Charlie wants me to look at him. I know he wants to try to calm me down, reassure me, or whatever he thinks I need right now. But the only thing that'll make me feel better is getting into the pool and swimming this off. Part of what we're also not talking about here is that since I'm a better swimmer than Charlie is, it's possible I could get into a school that rejects him, even though he makes way better grades. Even if there has to be summer school, which of course there can't be.

"I'll still help you, if you want," he finally says.

"What would really help would be if I could just challenge Woodham to a race. See who's so superior then."

Mainly I say this to take the attention away from Charlie's offer. Though it's nice he wants to help, I can't really picture the two of us, heads together in the library, doing something so boyfriend-girlfriendy. Sitting together at lunch is public enough; I didn't want to do it all, until I realized having someone to complain to, someone in the know about swim difficulties and lingo, helped take the edge off until it was time to be in the pool. For now I shrug without giving him an answer and chew big mouthfuls of my salad.

"A smackdown between you and Woodham would be pretty funny," he says finally. "In fact, I'd pay to see it."

And damn him—in spite of how pissed I am—that does make me laugh.

SimonTEEN

Simon & Schuster's **Simon Teen**
e-newsletter delivers current updates on
the hottest titles, exciting sweepstakes, and
exclusive content from your favorite authors.

Visit **TEEN.SimonandSchuster.com** to
sign up, post your thoughts. and find out what
every avid reader is talking about!